HIS MOTHERLESS LITTLE TWINS

BY
DIANNE DRAKE

MILLS & BOON®

First published in Great Britain 2010
Large Print edition 2010
Harlequin Mills & Boon Limited,
Eton House, 18-24 Paradise Road,
Richmond, Surrey TW9 1SR

© Dianne Despain 2010

ISBN: 978 0 263 21122 1

Harlequin Mills & Boon policy is to use papers that are
natural, renewable and recyclable products and made
from wood grown in sustainable forests. The logging and
manufacturing process conform to the legal environmental
regulations of the country of origin.

Printed and bound in Great Britain
by CPI Antony Rowe, Chippenham, Wiltshire

Now that her children have left home, **Dianne Drake** is finally finding the time to do some of the things she adores— gardening, cooking, reading, shopping for antiques. Her absolute passion in life, however, is adopting abandoned and abused animals. Right now Dianne and her husband Joel have a little menagerie of three dogs and two cats, but that's always subject to change. A former symphony orchestra member, Dianne now attends the symphony as a spectator several times a month and, when time permits, takes in an occasional football, basketball or hockey game.

Recent titles by the same author:

FOUND: A MOTHER FOR HIS SON
DR VELASCOS' UNEXPECTED BABY
THE WIFE HE'S BEEN WAITING FOR
A BOSS BEYOND COMPARE

CHAPTER ONE

"I'LL be there in thirty or forty minutes, and don't even think about going out on your own. It's too dangerous." Dinah Corday had been studying the *Welcome to White Elk* sign for the past ten minutes, creeping inch by inch down the main road into the little village, along with the rest of the jammed-up traffic. Right this very moment, her heavily pregnant sister, Angela, was on the verge of braving the spring storm to go and stay with a pregnant friend, and Dinah wanted to get to her before she did that. But the rising waters weren't being accommodating. Nothing was. "Just don't do it, OK? I know you want to be with her, and I'm doing the best I can to get to you, but it's crazy out here. So just be patient." Easy to say, not so easy to do under the circumstances.

Glancing up at the three mountain peaks,

Dinah sighed impatiently. The mountains looming over the valley, affectionately called the older, middle, and younger Sisters, were said to have magical powers. According to Ute Indian legend, they protected those in their shadow, and while she'd never given much credence to mystical things, she hoped that this one was true. Because Angela would *absolutely* go out in this flood to help a friend as surely as Dinah was stuck in the slow lane, getting more frustrated with each passing second.

Ahead, she saw people on the street running about in a congested knot like ants scattering after the demise of their anthill. Traffic was lined up bumper to bumper. Detour signs were being erected on the streets. Streetlights weren't working. And the wind was blowing so hard the water pooling in the gutters was flowing in small waves. "Promise me you're not going anywhere until I get there to take you. You're too far along…" A smile found its way to Dinah's lips. She was going to be an aunt in a little while. That was nice. Their family needed something good to happen to them for a change. It was overdue. "Just, please, stay there and take care of yourself. I'm on my way."

Angela assured her she wouldn't budge, but that didn't relieve Dinah's anxiety. Of course, that anxiety was pelting her from so many different directions these days, she feared turning around lest something else came hurtling at her. Today, though, her mind was on Angela. Nothing else mattered.

Except the traffic. That mattered, and she wanted to honk her horn, pound on her horn actually, but what good would it do? She wasn't the only one stuck in this mess and, most likely, everyone else had somewhere important they needed to be, too. So as the radio weather forecaster was predicting more rain, she crept forward like the rest of the people were doing, one car length at a time, while the waters outside were getting deeper.

After listening to another ten mind-numbing minutes of dire weather warnings, Dinah finally turned off the news station and dialed into a soft jazz station then leaned her head against the headrest, hoping to relax. She needed to be calm, not agitated, when she got to Angela. "Calm…" she muttered, while she studied the raindrops sliding their own little paths over her windshield.

Some hit and trailed down in a straight line, never veering off an imaginary course, while others meandered, winding in and out, joining with other raindrops to make fatter, more interesting trails. Yet some hit, bounced, and seemed to disappear before they had their chance to slide downward to a new, unknown destiny. That was her, she thought. Hitting, bouncing, disappearing from view before her trail carried her to where she wanted to be. Hers had always been a destiny of chance, or one out of her control, like the raindrops that splashed themselves into oblivion even with so many interesting choices ahead.

Raindrops and unknown destinies…

Well, so much for clearing her mind and relaxing, she thought, trying hard to let the mellow wail of the tenor sax coming from the radio lull her into a daze. Dulcet tones, honey notes, all slipping down into her soul. This was a good day to be lulled. But as she willed the easy mood on herself, trying to force calm to her soul for Angela's sake, a thud on her bumper from the vehicle behind cut off all hope of calmness, sending her car pitching straight into the bumper of the car ahead. Not a hard impact but definitely a jarring one.

Twisting, Dinah looked into her rearview mirror to catch a glimpse of the perpetrator, but all she saw was an up-close image of a truck's shiny silver bumper…and the truck was already backing away from her. Right off, she opened the car door, ready to hop out regardless of the rain and see to the damage, but the man behind her beat her to it by stopping then jumping from his truck and running forward. He was a big, imposing man in a bright yellow slicker, the dress of choice for most of the people she'd seen here so far. Except he didn't come forward to her door like she'd expected he would. Rather, he got as far as the front of his truck, surveyed his bumper then hers, and that was as far as he went.

"Any damage?" she shouted, wishing she had one of those yellow rain slickers.

If he answered, she didn't hear him. But the rain was noisy, so were the road noises. So, after she'd fumbled an umbrella from the back of her car and opened it overhead, she tried calling to him again. "You're not hurt, are you?"

He didn't answer this time, either, so she tried once more. Admittedly, getting a little perturbed. "Did it cause any damage?"

His only response was a wave on his way back to his truck…waving with one hand, clutching a cell phone to his ear in the other. "I can't stay," he yelled, and she did hear that. "Jason, the man in the car ahead of you, said he'll take care of it, and…" The rest of his words were gobbled in a clap of thunder, and by the time it had rumbled on through, he'd jumped back into his truck and pulled around, stopping briefly at the car in front of her.

"You arrogant…" she yelled, slamming shut her car door and marching straight forward to catch him before he sped away altogether. She didn't need this today. Just didn't need this. And now, with this added delay, she was even more worried that Angela would try to get out in this storm on her own.

"You OK, Jason?" the man from the truck called to the man in the car she'd hit, who was beginning to climb out of his front seat. He, too, was dressed in a yellow slicker.

"What about me?" Dinah yelled, catching up to his truck and running to the window on the driver's side. "Don't you want to know how I am?"

The man who'd hit her did turn around in his

seat, giving her a long, hard stare. "You're not hurt, are you?"

"No, but—"

"I'm sorry," he said. "But I can't deal with this right now. Like I told you before, Jason will take care of the details because I've got an emergency, and I've got to get back." He paused then smiled. "I'm really sorry about this."

He seemed sincere enough, his smile was… nice. But she didn't trust nice smiles, and sincerity was easy to fake. If anybody knew those two things, she did! Yet as she was about to shut out that nice smile altogether and demand he step out of the truck regardless of what his other obligations were, a gust of wind caught her umbrella, turned it inside out, then ripped it from her hands. Unfortunately, it tumbled end over end across the road, leaving Dinah standing in water up to her ankles, with her long, auburn hair soaked and shaggy, and nothing to protect her. She was barely even noticing the rain, though, because at this point she was too angry. "You can't just leave the scene," she yelled at the man. He was going to leave, though. That's what men did. They left. And she couldn't stop him.

Couldn't stop any of them. Father, husband, fiancé, brother-in-law, strangers…all alike.

Before the stranger pulled away, though, he handed an umbrella out the window to her. "I'm sorry, but I can't deal with this right now. So, please, step back. I don't want to splash you…" He took a good look at her waterlogged state and grimaced visibly. "Don't want to get you any wetter than you are."

Well, she could step in front of his truck and stop him, or grab hold of the handle on his door. But there was something in his eyes…a look she knew. Not a malicious one, not even a little mean-spirited. For an instant, something so deep there grabbed hold of her senses, willed her to step back. So she did, immediately regretting that, once again, she'd let herself be taken advantage of by a good-looker. In her life, trust amounted to betrayal. She almost counted on it, and that was a huge regret, too.

The proof of her regret was in the blow of black smoke from his tailpipe as he sped away from her, while she remained standing in the downpour, watching him, gripping his umbrella in a stranglehold, getting wetter and wetter.

* * *

"I'm glad Gabby has been such a good friend to you, especially since I haven't been of much use these past months," Dinah said to her sister.

Angela laid her hand on Dinah's. "Not your fault. We all have our problems to solve. And I've been doing fine here on my own. Good friends, good care. Nothing to worry about."

Except a cheating ski-bum of a husband who'd run away from Angela the moment he'd heard the word *pregnant*. "I'm your sister and I'm entitled to worry anyway. But like I said, I'm glad you've had Gabby here to help you get through." Dr. Gabrielle Evans. Angela's friend, and her doctor, who was on the verge of giving birth right this very moment, fully in labor. "So, how are you doing, Gabby?"

Gabby nodded, panted, grasped the edge of the bed while Angela wiped her forehead with a cool, damp cloth and Dinah positioned herself to see how dilated Gabby was. Dinah had been a pediatric nurse, but she'd had good experience in obstetrics. While there was supposed to be a doctor on the way to deliver this baby, and since taking Gabby to the hospital in this weather in her condition would be a crazy thing to do,

Gabby was ready to deliver this baby right here, right now, doctor or not. And it was beginning to look like Dinah might have to come out of her self-imposed retirement to bring the baby that Gabby was already calling Bryce into the world.

"Can I do anything else?" Angela asked.

"Just sit down and relax. I don't want you getting worked up and going into labor yourself," Dinah said, truly concerned about the effect the strain of all this excitement could have on her sister. Two women on the verge of motherhood. She envied them. Once, a long time ago, she'd thought that's what she'd wanted most in the world. But the marriage hadn't worked out, and she'd gone in another direction with her life. Then, years later, along had come Charles, the man she'd hoped would be…well, it didn't matter what she'd hoped. She'd been wrong about him, too.

Still, with all these babies coming into the world… "Relax, Gabby," she said, as another contraction gripped the woman. "I think this is going to be over with pretty soon. Bryce is in position and he's about to make his grand entrance."

"I hope so," Gabby forced out as the contraction came to an end. "Because I'm tired of this part of it."

Dinah laughed. "But you'll be a much better obstetrician for having gone through it yourself. At least, that sounds good in theory, doesn't it? And now, when you tell your patients you understand, you really will." She laid a hand on Gabrielle's belly, felt the amazing stirring of a new life just under her fingertips. Suddenly, she was glad she was there, being part of it.

"Angela tells me you've quit nursing," Gabby gasped. She was finally relaxing back into her pillows. But not for long, if her progression towards the birth remained this consistent.

"For now. I came here to cook for Angela while she's off on maternity leave, then I'll decide what I want to do after that." Dinah's sister was the executive chef at the lodge on one of the Three Sisters and, like Angela, Dinah had also gone to culinary school. But she'd quit part way through to go into nursing. Culinary school, like her first marriage, had been a hasty decision, and not the right one. But nursing…she loved it. Missed it already.

Right now, though, with so many unresolved issues, she had to step away. The reasons were complicated, and she didn't trust herself to make the right decision while she was still feeling the sting.

"I'm glad you can deliver a baby, because I didn't want to do this by myself," Gabby said, as another contraction hit. "And I was afraid I might have to."

The contractions were coming fast. In the hour they'd been there they'd sped up considerably, telling Dinah that Gabby was in an unusually fast labor. It was time to get her in position and hope the doctor arrived in time, that the floodwaters outside wouldn't hold him back. Or do what she had to do if he couldn't get through.

Funny, how she'd quit nursing, not sure she could ever go back to it. Yet here she was, doing what she'd promised herself she wouldn't do again until her life was in better control, if that were even possible now, and wondering if she'd made yet another bad choice by leaving the thing she most loved doing.

Which was the reason she'd had to leave. Because these days she was just…confused.

And sad.

* * *

Dr. Neil Ranard arrived in time to deliver Gabby's baby, and the first thing Dinah saw was just how much he loved Gabby. Angela had already told her that the baby wasn't Neil's, but deep down Dinah believed that Neil would raise that baby, because the look she saw in Gabby's eyes the instant Neil ran into the room said everything. It was nice. But what was even nicer was seeing that it was out there…true love did exist. Maybe not for her. But it was nice for others who were luckier than she was. Or smarter.

"Just one more push, Gabrielle," Neil urged. "That's all I need. One more push and you're a mother!"

Dinah propped Gabby up into position, enjoying what she was doing, even if it was a little outside her nursing expertise. It was good to be useful again, good to help. For a while, the ache of missing it was eased a little.

"Bear down, Gabrielle, and push," Neil said.

"I am," Gabby gasped.

"Breathe," Dinah said. "Come on, Gabby. Take a deep breath, then push that baby out."

"He's waiting for you, Gabrielle," Neil prompted. "Bryce Evans is waiting for you."

Gabby bore down for a final time as Dinah helped her through her final contraction. Then, suddenly, it was over. Bryce was here. But…dear God, he was blue. Dinah saw it immediately, felt her stomach roil, and exchanged a quick look with Dr. Ranard. A look that said everything.

"Let me see him," Gabby said to the deathly quiet room. "My baby…"

Dinah eased Gabby back into a flat position on the bed, propped a pillow under her head then ran to the end of the bed to see what she could do for Dr. Ranard. Or for the limp little newborn in his hands.

"He isn't crying," Gabby gasped, fighting to sit back up. Thrashing wildly, she was trying to toss off the sheets covering her. "Neil, he isn't crying! What's wrong?"

"Take care of Gabrielle," Neil whispered to Dinah. "Don't let her see…"

Even before he'd finished speaking, Dinah positioned herself between Neil and the bed, so Gabby couldn't see Neil's resuscitation attempts and the next minutes went by in a blur as she tried to calm the grief-stricken mother and help the doctor with the baby.

"Did he aspirate?" Dinah whispered to Neil, although she didn't believe so. As a pediatric trauma nurse, her first guess was something cardiac, or related to the lungs, judging from the baby's listlessness and bluish pallor.

Not again! Dear God, not again! *How could she face another newborn dying?* Bryce had a chance to survive, Molly never had. She had to stay focused on that! *This* was the baby who needed her now. This was Bryce Evans, not Molly Collins.

"Is he alive?" Gabby screamed. "Neil, you've got to tell me, is he alive? I've got to get to my baby." She launched herself up, but Dinah stopped her, applying a firm hand into her shoulder.

More minutes ticked by, and Bryce still struggled. Outside, the floods were getting worse. The hospital had promised to send a medic with supplies, but each second seemed like an hour— a frantic, futile hour in which they were losing a battle. All the while, Dinah was forced to physically restrain Gabby from flying across the room to Neil. Neil didn't need that. Neither did the baby, who was not improving. She hated doing that. Hated it more than anyone could imagine, because she knew how it felt. Knew how Gabby felt, needing desperately to get there and being pulled away against her will.

Then suddenly Bryce quit breathing and Dinah was thrown back to that day when baby Molly had died in her arms. Regret, instant and brutal, assaulted her, causing a feeling of panic to rise up and strangle the breath from her. For a moment she was back there in that hospital room, struggling and crying like Gabby was, begging them not to take Molly away from her.

"Is that CPR?" Gabby cried, snapping Dinah back into the moment. "Is Neil giving him CPR?"

More minutes blurred in the battle as Bryce began showing signs of reviving. Bryce had Neil to fight for him, and Neil loved him. That was so obvious. There'd been no one to care for Molly. No one had loved her. Except *her*. And in the end, that hadn't been enough.

Now the melancholia threatened to pull her under.

"You!"

The voice from the doorway startled Dinah from her thoughts of Molly, and she jumped.

"You!" she snapped right back at him. Of all the people who could have come, it would be *him*, Mr Hit-and-Run himself. And he was standing there, holding out a pediatric oxygen mask.

Dinah yanked the mask from the man's hands, and rushed to put it on Bryce. Then the medic opened the oxygen tank valve once the mask was in place.

"It was a slight tap," he said. "No damage."

"And you didn't stop to see if you'd damaged my car, or injured me," Dinah snarled under her breath to keep her problem with this man quiet, as she pulled a pediatric IV needle from the bag of supplies he'd brought and prepared to insert it into the baby's thread-sized vein. It's what she did, no one had to tell her. No one had to help her. It's simply what she was trained to do, and did instinctively.

As she set about her work, she noticed that Bryce was already pinking up. Not enough to think he was out of danger, but enough to be encouraged.

"You take care of Gabby," the medic whispered to Neil. "She needs you right now, and I'll take care of the baby."

Neil handed off the responsibility without hesitation, and the two men exchanged quiet words for a moment. "Thanks, Eric," Neil finally said, then ran to Gabrielle.

"You're a doctor?" Dinah asked.

"Eric Ramsey, pediatric surgeon, with a secondary in trauma." He pulled a bag of fluid from his supplies and hooked it to the line once Dinah had inserted the IV catheter. Then he adjusted the drip of fluid into the baby's veins, and immediately listened to Bryce's chest.

The next few minutes they worked side by side in total silence, both doing what they knew needed to be done to stabilize their tiny patient.

"He's a fighter," Eric finally pronounced, turning around to Gabby. "We've got him as stabilized as we can, so now I need to get him to the hospital. But I want you to hold him first."

She took her baby, and the way she clung to him nearly broke Dinah's heart. No one had loved little Molly like that…someone should have. She couldn't bear watching, the memories were too painful and she had to turn away.

"I was in a hurry…emergency." Eric stepped up behind her. "Otherwise I wouldn't have driven off like that."

"What?" Dinah asked.

"The accident. I had an emergency. I'm sorry, but—"

"But we all do what we have to do, don't we?" she whispered. "It doesn't matter what we do to the people around us, as long as it's good for us. I get it. You don't need to apologize."

"Yes, I do." Eric took a step back, shook his head. "Look, Neil thinks Bryce's problem might be TGV." Transposition of the great vessels, where the two main arteries leaving the heart were reversed. Normally, blood from the heart's right ventricle was carried by the pulmonary artery to the lungs, and blood from the left ventricle was taken by the aorta to the body. In the case of TGV, it was just the opposite, leaving the oxygenated blood meant to circulate through the body being pumped back into the lungs. "And at this point, I have no reason to disagree because the symptoms fit. Things may turn out differently once we get the baby—"

"You think it's TGV, too?" Dinah's mind raced through the procedures. There would be a first surgery, called a septostomy, to do an immediate, life-saving correction. In that, a hole was literally opened up to allow better flow of the blood. It was a temporary measure to be followed by another surgery to make the permanent repair. She'd treated babies who'd had the surgery, seen good outcomes, seen bad outcomes.

"You'll drive."

"Where?" she asked.

"To the hospital. You'll drive, I'll take care of the baby."

The tension in the cab of the truck was so thick Dinah could have sliced through it with a scalpel. They'd been en route five minutes now, taking a back road that skirted the valley. It was muddy and slick, but it wasn't washed out. And it was on higher ground, which was what made it a safer bet than taking the road down below the house, where the water was at least as high as the bottom of the truck door. Flash-flood warnings were out now, and all the lower roads were being closed. So she and Eric were driving along what amounted to little more than a fire trail, and Dinah was so nervous that her grip on the steering-wheel hurt. All the while, neither she nor Eric had spoken a word to each other since his initial instruction to her on getting to the hospital.

Yet in his defense, Eric was busy tending to Bryce, holding him in his lap and continually checking his pulse, his respiratory status, being so tender, so caring with him while she was fighting to stay straight and to avoid the bumps and ruts, most of which she couldn't even see.

It crossed her mind that he was the doctor Molly should have had. He would have cared more than Charles had, even when hope had died. Charles, the man she'd almost married. How could she have been so wrong about him? Even thinking about it made her cringe.

Once or twice, Bryce let out a little cry then settled down again. And once or twice her heart lurched. Under the best of circumstances, this was a difficult situation. These *weren't* the best of circumstances, and she fretted about the outcome every inch of the way to the hospital.

"Are you competent?" she finally asked, not at all sorry to be so blunt. Truth was, she wanted to hear his voice, feel some reassurance that he could handle this situation and make everything right for the baby.

"Competent at what?"

"Your medical skills. Are you a good doctor?"

"I've been told that's the case." He twisted slightly in his seat to look at her. "But, then, everyone is entitled to his, *or her*, opinion, I suppose."

"I suppose," Dinah muttered. Something about this man put her in a very bad mood. Something about every man had put her in a bad mood lately, but this one in particular made her shiver. Shiver with anger was what it was, which she didn't like one little bit. Didn't like any reaction in her caused by any man. And didn't trust herself enough to know the distinctions.

"Are *you* competent?" he asked in return, the slightest trace of a smile crinkling his lips.

She was going to ignore that smile. Totally ignore it and pretend she hadn't even seen it. "Competent at what?"

"Being a nurse."

"I'm not a nurse." Keeping her voice noncommittal wasn't easy, but she did it, and did it so well she nearly believed her own words. Still, those words hurt, and the wound still bled. "I'm a cook. Here to take over for my sister when she's on maternity leave."

"A cook with good skills in labor and delivery, as well as CPR. And you did a mighty fine job of getting that IV needle into a newborn, which is not easy, especially when the newborn is so sick. So, did they teach you those things in culinary school?"

He was smiling fully now. The man actually had the audacity to sit there and smile at her. But she was still going to ignore it. Had to be impervious… Couldn't get distracted. "Did they teach you your bad manners in medical school?"

"If I apologized for the accident again, would that make things better between us?"

"Why do things have to be better between us?" she asked, then hastily added, "But you do owe me a sincere apology and not one that's meant only to get you away from me as quickly as possible."

"Look, I told you I was in a hurry. I'm sorry I hit you, sorry I ran off and left you there, but in case you haven't noticed, the town is going crazy. We're flooding, the areas below us are submerging, the hospital is full of people with nowhere to go, some of them have injuries. I had to get to the emergency department, and stopping for something that amounted to nothing was a waste of my time."

"And I thought White Elk was going to be civil," she snapped. Gripping the steering-wheel more from anger than nervousness, she kept her eyes fixed straight ahead. "But I was wrong."

"No, you weren't wrong. Had it been any other time, under any other circumstances, I would have stopped and given you that sincere apology. But you were...not a priority. Getting to the hospital was."

OK, she understood that. And maybe he was right. No, he *was* right. And she was overreacting. Which she'd been accused of doing a lot of lately. "It's been a bad day," she conceded. A bad day, a worse week and an even worse month. And everything was still spiraling downward. "I should be the one apologizing to you."

"No apologies necessary. And you're right, it's been a bad day for everyone." He glanced down at his tiny patient. "But mostly for him."

Suddenly, all the anger and frustration drained right out of her. Sick children had a way of putting everything else into proper perspective, had a way of bringing everything else around them to a grinding halt. "How's he doing?"

"Struggling. But fighting. He's one tough little boy. So, are you a friend of Gabby's?"

"No, I only met her today, right before I helped deliver Bryce. But I'm Angela Blanchard's sister. And I'm really here to take over for her in the kitchen."

"Funny. I would have sworn you were a nurse. A damn good one, if I had to make a bet on it."

"I was a pediatric nurse and, yes, I like to think I was a damn good one, but that's in the past," she said. "I burned out." That wasn't the truth, but it was an easy explanation and people didn't question it.

"Sorry to hear that. Especially since you seem so…passionate about it. That's medicine's loss."

He sounded genuinely sorry, which surprised her. When she'd tendered her resignation, no one had even tried talking her out of her decision to quit. Then, when she'd closed all those doors on her life and walked away, no one had been sorry to see her go. No one had even blinked. But by then she'd become an awkward moment for the man who was supposed to love her. He was an upwardly mobile doctor, she was a downwardly spiraling nurse he found quite easy to leave. *You're too emotional, Dinah. You overreacted. Got yourself too involved in something you had no business getting involved in. Maybe you should have stayed in cooking school.*

But she believed Eric Ramsey sounded sorry she'd left nursing.

Except she didn't trust herself to believe anything. Not anymore.

CHAPTER TWO

"You didn't, by any chance, ever assist in a septostomy did you?" Eric asked, handing the baby over to the two nurses who'd run to greet them when they'd pulled up to White Elk Hospital's front door.

"I've seen them done. And taken care of the patient afterwards. Why?"

"We're short-staffed right now, and I could use you in the operating room if you've got the experience."

"I do have the experience," she said hesitantly. Her preference would have been helping the volunteer crews who were busy sandbagging the hospital, trying to keep the flood waters back from it. That was something she could do, something that wouldn't remind her of how much she ached for a career that hurt her so deeply.

"Then I need your experience. Normally, I'd have another doctor in there, but he's driving Gabby and your sister to the hospital right now, and everybody else is tied up. I can grab our nurse practitioner, Fallon, and she's competent in surgery, but her skills are more needed in co-ordinating everything else that's going on. So if you know your way around the operating room…"

He actually wanted her in surgery? She was flattered, but she'd walked away from being a nurse. Not because she didn't care, but because she cared too much. By rights, she should have turned him down and under most other circumstances she would have. But there was a baby who needed her…*another baby*…

"*Please* assist me. I have a very sick little boy who needs surgery, but if all my qualified staff are busy elsewhere, his surgery may have to be put off until we have the right combination of people free. You know what that could mean."

Yes, she did know. When he put it that way, what was she supposed to do? How could she walk away from Bryce the way everybody had walked away from little Molly? "OK, I was more than a staff nurse. I was the head pediatric trauma nurse in my hospital. Just in case you want to know, or check my qualifications."

"You wear your qualifications for everybody to see," he said. "And I'm a pretty good judge of that."

Better judge than she was. Once upon a time she wouldn't have hesitated. Now she wasn't sure. "Where do I scrub in?" she asked on a disheartened sigh.

Eric pointed her in the direction of the surgery. "What's your name, by the way?"

"None of your business," she snapped. If he knew her name, it got personal, and she wasn't doing personal again. Personal hurt. It devastated. And she was tired of the pain.

Eric laughed. "When you scrub, I'd suggest you use cold water. Might cool you down a little."

Well, he generally didn't like his women so feisty. Lord knew, nothing about Patricia had been feisty. She'd been the model of cool, calm composure in everything. Always smiling, always happy, Patricia had been perfect. Maybe too perfect for the likes of him. But this woman…she was spunky, boisterous, argumentative, and in just an hour or so of knowing her, she'd raised her voice to him more than his wife had in all the years they'd been together.

Yet there was something about her that wouldn't let him look away. Drawn like a moth to the flame...that's the thought that kept running through his head. But didn't the moth usually get burned to a crisp?

This woman was all fire. Get too close and you were sure to get burned. But she was on his mind anyway, and it had nothing to do with his expectations of a pediatric trauma nurse, and everything to do with feelings he'd vowed he'd never let happen. He'd had a perfect marriage once. Anything else would fall short.

Besides, he had two little daughters to consider. In his life, they mattered more than anything else and the thought of putting them through a life-changing adjustment scared him. They were good the way they were...all three of them. Very good.

His thoughts were interrupted by the arrival of Neil Ranard, desperate for news about Gabby's son.

"You look bothered," Neil Ranard said, as Eric scrubbed. "Is it about Bryce?"

Eric shook his head, but didn't answer right away, because what bothered him was the disloyalty he was suddenly feeling, thinking about the beautiful nurse the way he was. He had no business looking at another woman, and the wedding band on his left ring finger was a shining testament to that. "No, he's stable right now. Doing pretty well last time I checked. The good news is that once we've done this first procedure he should be stable enough to be transferred to get the help we simply can't provide here."

"Gabby and I have every faith in your abilities, Eric. Neither of us would want anyone else helping Bryce right now."

"I'll do my very best not to let you down."

"I know you will. So if you're not too worried about Bryce right now, what is bugging you? Hold on, this wouldn't be about working with Dinah Corday, would it?"

This time he didn't bother shaking his head, as the guilt was beginning to consume him. Because, yes, it was about Dinah—so that was her name! She intrigued him. And she was sexy as hell. Something he had no right noticing.

"Well, she's a looker," Neil conceded. "And

even though we've only worked together once, she's one of the best nurses I've ever dealt with. So, which of those two qualities is distracting you? Because it's got to be one of them, since you don't know anything else about her."

"I'm not distracted," Eric snapped. "I'm concentrating, and you're breaking my concentration."

Neil laughed. "I think your concentration was broken before I came in here, and it's got nothing to do with anything medical."

"It's not what you think," Eric denied. "I don't have time, and you know that. Between my job, and my rescue duties, and especially with the twins…" He shook his head as he backed away from the sink, arms up, water dripping down to his elbows. "I don't have time, no matter how much she…or any other woman…breaks my concentration. So I'm not going to let it happen, simple as that."

"Look, Eric. I know you were totally devoted to Patricia, but she's been gone for five years, and I don't think she would have wanted you putting yourself through this. She would have wanted you to be happy again. To find a new life for yourself…something in addition to your work.

And that would include finding someone else to share that life. But you haven't even taken a woman out for a simple dinner, have you?"

"Once or twice." Truth was, after Patricia had died, he'd lost interest. Hadn't found it again, either, because in his heart he was still a married man.

"Look, I know it's not easy. Believe me, if anyone knows how hard it is to pick up the pieces and move on, it's me. After my marriage broke up…" He paused, shrugged, then smiled. "But I'm working it out with Gabrielle now, and I think we're going to get married. Which shows how easily the past becomes just that—the past—when the right future opens up to you. So keep yourself open to the possibilities, because you deserve to find some happiness. If not with Dinah Corday, then with someone else."

"What if I don't want to open myself up to them? I mean, what if I like keeping myself shut off?" Eric spun away from Neil and pushed through the surgical door, stepping directly into the gown the surgical tech was holding up for him. He was back in the moment now, back in the zone. That's what always happened the instant he stepped into surgery and right now, even though the most gorgeous pair of brown eyes he'd ever seen in his life were staring over a surgical mask at him, he was focused on starting the procedure to save Bryce Evans's life.

But as he stepped up to the table, for one fleeting moment the only thing he saw in front of him were those eyes. Beautiful eyes. Distracting. Then he blocked them out, and cleared his throat. "Let's go over the surgical check list before we start."

Well, if this hadn't been quite the day! She'd helped deliver one baby, helped resuscitate that baby, and had then assisted in his surgery. All that, plus dodging a flood. By all rights, she should have been tired, exhausted, ready to find a quiet corner somewhere, put her feet up and take a nap. That's probably what she'd do in a little while, when she finally wound down. But right now she felt alive. Invigorated. It had been three long, difficult weeks since Molly's death. Three weeks to doubt herself, three weeks being berated for caring by the man who had claimed to love her. Three weeks of agony and self-doubt.

Yet in the span of only a few hours now, it was like she'd been sustained again. Sustained, validated. Made to feel normal. Of course, it would all be over with once she stepped outside the confines of this hospital. So she wanted to bask a while longer in a place where she felt like she belonged, to linger in the good feelings. Besides, she felt safe here. She'd never, ever in her life set foot into such a tiny, crazy hospital as this one, where trauma doctors had second careers as surgeons and third careers as heads of search and rescue, and where doctors still made house calls and invited total strangers into the surgery. As mixed up as it all seemed, she liked it so much she could almost picture herself belonging here, and that was a nice feeling she wanted to last for a while longer because, to be honest, she doubted she'd ever get it back.

Creeping into the intensive care nursery, where the lights were dimmed for the sleeping hours, and the green, glowing trace of baby Bryce's heartbeat on the cardiac monitor next to his bed illuminated the area like an eerie beacon, Dinah stopped halfway to the crib to admire the miracle baby lying there, breathing easily and sleeping peacefully. All was right in his world and he had no idea how people had scrambled to save his life today, how they'd put their own lives at risk to save him. Neither had he any idea how many people had already crept in to see how he was doing, or hovered outside the door, worrying about him. He had no idea that things weren't perfect, and that's the way it should always be in a child's world. Molly should have had a chance at that, if even for a moment.

Dinah loved children, loved taking care of them, loved the innocence of the smiles and giggles. She'd fallen in love with Molly. Abandoned at birth because of overwhelming disabilities, her birth mother had simply walked away. Never looked back. And had left a precious child to die alone in an impersonal hospital nursery where the duty nurses took good care, but didn't truly care. No child should ever be alone that way, and she'd made sure Molly had never been alone.

It had reawakened something in her. A longing. And watching Bryce now reminded her of the all things he would have ahead of him, things Molly wouldn't have. She wouldn't have gone home from the hospital, wouldn't have slept in a crib, wouldn't have had toys to play with. All those weeks sitting with Molly in the hospital, holding her, singing to her, she'd wanted to pretend things could be normal for the child, but she'd known... as a nurse, she'd known. All those weeks with Charles calling her crazy for getting involved. Hopeless was what he'd called Molly. But Dinah had never seen hopeless. All she'd seen had been a sick child who'd had no one but her.

How could she have been so wrong about Charles? He was a pediatrician. He was supposed to love children, no matter what their condition. Through Molly, what she'd come to know had been a man who could barely tolerate them.

How could she have been so blind?

Now, watching Bryce, and feeling so connected to him, the longing to be part of something so good was stirring again. It would be nice to sit and cradle him in her arms the way she had Molly, to whisper motherly things in his tiny ear. It was a feeling that scared her, though, because she knew the pain of loss when it ended. It was unbearable. So deep and profound nothing could touch it or make it better.

Not ever.

With her marriage to Damien, shortly after she'd graduated from nursing school, she'd wanted all the right things—the nice little house with a white picket fence. Wanted to bake pies for her husband and cool them on the windowsill in the afternoon so their sweet aromas would waft down to him as he came home from work. Wanted children playing in the yard. Wanted to snuggle with him in the evening after the children were in bed, and talk about the things that were interesting to no one but themselves—how their days had been, who they'd met on the street, what they were going to do tomorrow, and next week and next year. But that was a dream life that hadn't come true as Damien had been bored with their daydreams by the end of their first year together and already working on a way to find his life with someone else. And here she was now, at thirty-four, fresh from the last daydream fiasco with Charles, older but, apparently, not much wiser.

Well, experience was the best teacher. Maybe she had a tendency to let her heart rule her head, but this time her head was fastened on better. Avoid relationships and the problems didn't happen.

"He looks so peaceful, you wouldn't know what he's just gone through, would you?" Eric asked.

"Eric!" she gasped, startled that he'd been able to sneak up on her like that. She'd been too lost in the daydream she didn't want to have, too caught up in something she couldn't allow herself, and this lapse in judgment had everything to do with him. Not that he would be interested in her that way. Yet he was practically hanging over her shoulder now. Standing much too close. So close, in fact, that the scent of soap on his skin threatened to tip her right back into her daydream.

As a preventative to the thoughts trying to creep in, Dinah moved round to the other side of the baby's crib, laid her hands on the raised rails and relaxed a little. She was safe here, keeping so many physical obstacles between her and Eric, even if Eric didn't know what she was doing, or how she was feeling, being so close to him. "Babies are resilient. Much more than we are, I think."

"Is that why you chose pediatrics?" he asked.

"Actually, my most recent choice was a kitchen in a ski lodge." It was a blatant dodge, but she didn't want to talk about it, didn't want to look up at him for fear he could find the answers he was seeking in her eyes. And they were there, she was sure of it.

"Before that."

"In my life, *before that* doesn't matter," she said, her voice now a whisper. "I've had a few of those and now I am what I am in the moment. Don't expect anything else." He was going to respond to that. In fact, she was so sure of it she practically held her breath waiting for it, but when he didn't, Dinah finally did look up. "No response?" she asked. "No pithy little comeback?"

"Something I learned a long time ago is that when people drop those kinds of explosive statements, it's best to back away. If they want to explain it, they will. If they don't, you're at a safe distance." He grinned. "Right now, I like the safety in this distance."

"I appreciate that," she said. And truly she did. There was no point starting a new life and blurting out all the unhappy parts of the old one every time the opportunity arose. While she wasn't really here to make new friends, or find a new start, she did want to make the most of the next few weeks, especially with the people she might see occasionally. And Eric Ramsey…she had a hunch she'd be seeing him again. Nothing social, nothing even very friendly. But there was something about saving a life together that pulled people closer, at least for a little while. Besides, Eric might be here when she came to check on little Bryce. So why beat him over the head with all her baggage for what would amount to a few casual moments here and there? "People don't know when to observe boundaries. They step over the line, assume they have rights where they really have none, and the next thing you know…" They're cheating on you, or walking out of your life. "Thank you, Eric."

"Thank you, Dinah." He spoke the words, but even in the dim light his eyes said more. So much more it startled her.

"I…um…I'm glad we were able to work together." His intense stare on her was unsettling. It was making her nervous. Causing her hands to shake. Yet she couldn't look away. Wanted to, but could not. "And I'm even more glad that things are going to work out for Bryce and Gabby." The conversation was turning just plain awkward now. There was nothing more to say except goodbye. Yet she didn't want to. Not yet. "Anyway… I, um…I guess this is goodbye. I need to get back to Angela, and um…" Was it hot in here? Because she was suddenly burning up. "I'm sure we'll see each other again while I'm in White Elk. So…" She needed a fan, her cheeks were blazing so furiously. "So, I'll see you around."

"See you around, Dinah Corday." He winked.

Eric's voice so sexy she went weak in the knees. Maybe she was tired. Everything was catching up to her and a few hours' sleep would take care of whatever this was coming over her. Yes, that had to be it. She was tired. Her body was giving out on her. "Around," she repeated, not making the slightest move to leave.

Suddenly, Eric was around on her side of the crib, and before she realized what was going on…or maybe she did realize what was going on and didn't want to do anything about it, she was in his arms. Locked into a kiss. Deep, urgent. Lips pressed so hard she could scarcely find breath. Her arms snaked up around his neck like they'd done it a thousand times before, and her body willed itself into a tight press to his, until she could almost feel corded muscles, almost find her way deep inside him. But as suddenly as the kiss had started, it stopped. His awareness…her awareness… What they were doing shoved them apart with such a force that it was like a physical punch, one that knocked her back.

Of all the crazy, stupid things to do! How could she have?

And how could her knees still be wobbly from the force of one simple kiss?

Except it hadn't been simple. Nothing about that kiss had been simple, and she was reeling to find an explanation. What had caused it? Had it been about two people caught up in the moment, two people who'd waged the battle together and won? A kiss of celebration?

Yes, that made sense. A kiss of celebration. That sounded feasible, or feasible enough. Plus, she was tired. Exhausted.

Except it was a kiss that shook her to the very core. One that made her knees wobble so hard she had to grab hold of the crib rails. "I…I didn't mean for that to happen," she stammered. "I've been accused of overreacting in emotional situations, and I think you've just seen that." Although she'd never, ever, kissed anyone so impulsively before. "Sorry." Lame excuse, but it was the best she could do. "So, it's been a long day. Like I said, I want to go spend some time with Angela, see if we can get up to the lodge so I can finally get settled in."

If ever there was a perfect time to make her exit, this was it. Eric hadn't said word, not one single word in reaction. So all she had to do was grab up what was left of her strength, forget her dignity, since that was long gone, hold her head high and walk out the door. Except her feet wouldn't move when she tried. Both were planted firmly to the tiled floor and going nowhere soon. Or maybe she simply didn't want to walk around him and risk falling into his arms again.

Eric didn't move either. And his face, even in the dim lights, was painted with sheer panic and perplexity. A sure sign of what he was thinking, which embarrassed her even more. It wasn't like she'd kissed every doctor with whom she'd shared a victory, because she hadn't. Yet one minute she was telling him to keep his boundaries, and the next minute those boundaries had tumbled down—that emotional overreaction Charles had berated her for. Maybe Charles had been right when he'd told her she was more suited, emotionally, to the kitchen. "Look, Eric, I shouldn't have—"

He thrust out his hand to stop her. Still scowling. Still perplexed. "What you did today with Bryce was nothing short of amazing, Dinah. I don't want to take anything away from that."

In the uncomfortable moment between them, she shrugged for the lack of a better response.

"And for the record, I'm sorry about the way I behaved after we had that little collision on the road."

"It doesn't matter," she managed, barely sounding any more steady than she felt.

"But it does. I'd had one hell of a morning, between the floods and the hospital. My twin girls have been sick, and I had to leave to make sure they were safe, then I had to get back to the hospital right away. But they were frightened. Wanted me to stay home with them. Cried, begged. And nothing pulls at your heart harder than two little girls begging for you to stay. So I stayed longer than I should have, was distracted when I finally did leave, and you…" He chuckled nervously, "Well, you know the rest of the story."

The rest of the story? Did he mean the part where she'd just kissed a married man? Somehow, with the casual way he acted around her, she wouldn't have guessed that about him. Who was she kidding, though? Her life was a testament to not guessing the right thing. And the right thing with Eric was that he wasn't only married, but married with children. A man with huge entanglements.

Well, something in her life was finally simple. One kiss, *and he'd been a willing part of it*, was where it ended. Actually, she was glad about that because her judgment wasn't going to be tested on this. They'd met their final boundary. Nothing came after it. Period. No doubts, no questions, nothing to wonder about. "How old are they?" she asked, at last finding enough strength to push her toward the door. "Your twins? How old are they?"

"Five, going on twenty-one. Spoiled rotten, and I'm not ashamed to admit it."

"Their names?" she asked, backing her way around Eric, keeping herself well clear of him as he stood at the end of the crib.

"Pippa. She's older by nine minutes, and she's the outgoing one. My little extrovert who can't stay out of trouble. And Paige, my very serious introvert who tends to be more clingy than anything."

By the time she got to the door leading to the hall, she half expected Eric to flip a photo wallet out of his pocket, like a kiss followed by a trip through the family archives was all in a day's work for him. But he didn't. Rather, he turned around, popped his stethoscope into his ears and had a good look at Bryce. Checked his breath sounds, his heart, his reflexes, probably glad for that whole awkward episode to be over with.

That's when Dinah escaped.

"Don't let me keep you from your wife any longer," she bit out as she fled the ICU. She made it to the hall, got halfway down it and sagged against the wall. What was she doing? How could she have failed to notice the ring on his finger? And how, even now, knowing what she did about Eric Ramsey, was his kiss was still lingering on her lips? It burned all the way through her, and as she raised her fingers to her lips, she knew it would linger a while longer. Against her will. Or maybe because of her will.

For a moment, she'd thought Eric was different. But he was like the rest of them, wasn't he? Her father who'd walked out on this family, her husband who'd cheated on her, her fiancé who'd seen a weakness in her and exploited it. Well, she'd been gullible again. It was her history. Her habit. They spoke, she believed, she got hurt.

The masses of humanity in the hall were cloying, as she regained enough strength to fight her way through them to get to her sister. So many people with no place to go, people reaching out, people in pain. But Dinah was in her own unbelievable pain, and she didn't see them all through the tears stinging her eyes. She was hurt, angry, but mostly humiliated. Her fault entirely. She had to get away. Had to find Angela and get out of there. But she was almost half the way to the waiting area when Eric caught up to her.

"Dinah!" he yelled over the crowd.

She heard him, but didn't stop.

"Dinah!" he yelled again, catching up to her and falling into step. "Did you think I'd leave my wife at home with the girls while I was out hitting on you? Is that why you ran out? Because you thought I was…" He glanced down at the ring on his finger. "That I'd kiss you the way I did if I was…"

She tried to twist away from him and go the other direction, but Eric stepped in front of her then stepped in front of her again when she turned yet another way. "Look, Eric. I'll give you credit where it's due. You're a good doctor. But other than that, you do what you have to do, as long as it doesn't involve me. OK? I don't like men like you. No, let me restate that. I *hate* men like you, and I pity the women who keep falling for them because the result is always the same no matter how much they believe they're the one who will finally change him, finally tame the beast in him. Men like you don't tame. Once you've had a taste of what it's like to step outside the bounds of normal decency, you don't step back in. So, leave me alone. We've done what we had to do, and there's no reason to continue… anything."

Deep breath, Dinah, she kept telling herself. *Calm down.* This wasn't Damien Corday, her husband, who'd had the decency to wait six months into their marriage before cheating on her. It wasn't her father, a man who'd left his family because it hadn't been the family he'd wanted. Wasn't even Charles Lansing who'd turned on her in such a profound, hurtful way. This was Eric Ramsey, who was trying to cheat on Mrs. Eric Ramsey. Yes, pity the poor wife. But this time it was truly none of her business.

"Do I get to defend myself?"

"Against what?" Dinah snapped. She wouldn't look up at him, wouldn't take a long, slow journey into those gorgeous brown eyes because if she did she might do something stupid, like believe him. And the last thing she ever intended to do again was believe anything any man had to say. Sure, it was reactionary, but she had good cause to react the way she did.

"Against your accusations. You get to fling them at me, so I should have the opportunity to deflect them. To defend myself."

"I don't care what you have to say, Eric, because I've heard…*everything*. All the excuses, all the explanations. All the lies. There's nothing new under the sun, you know."

He opened his mouth to speak, to compound his lie, to make an even bigger fool of her, but at that very same moment a tiny figure in a pink rain slicker came running through the hall, directly to Eric, followed by an identical little figure in another pink rain slicker.

"Daddy!" Eric spun to see them, then braced himself against the inevitable as both little girls launched themselves into his arms at the very same time.

Galoshes halfway to their knees, rain slickers all the way down to the galoshes, rain hats covering up most of their faces, it was hard to see the little girls, but Dinah's heart did pound a little harder as Eric went down on one knee and scooped them both up into his embrace. They were giggling and laughing and splashing him with water dripping from their slickers, almost knocking him flat on his back in their exuberance.

"OK, girls," their mother said, coming up from behind. "I told you not to overwhelm your father. Remember he's been doing a very difficult surgery, and he's tired."

"But we brought him cookies," one of the girls cried.

"We've been baking," the woman Dinah took

to be Eric's wife said. "And baking, and baking. They were bored, and they missed you."

"Well, you know how I love your cookies!" Eric exclaimed, extricating himself from the girls and standing up. Once he was fully upright, both girls immediately latched on to him again, one girl holding on to each of his legs.

"Are you coming home now, Daddy?" one of the girls asked.

"Sorry, but I can't leave here yet. We're too busy. Too many people still coming in and you know Daddy has to stay here and take care of them."

"Then can we stay here and help?" the girls cried in unison. "Please, Daddy, can we stay?"

He looked at the woman, who shrugged. "I'm going to sit with Gabby, and Debbie's coming in shortly to look after the girls. So it's fine with me if they stay for a while," she said. "Maybe you can take a break with them later on?"

"How can I say no to taking a break with my two best girls?" Eric said. He took hold of the brims of both their rain hats and shoved them up. "But first I want you to say hello to Dinah Corday. She's the nurse who helped me in surgery today. The surgery I did on Dr. Evans's baby."

Totally unaware of her presence there, in this cozy family scene, until they spun to face her, they both ran immediately to Dinah and grabbed her like she was their long-lost friend. "Hello," she said tentatively.

"Hello," they said in unison. "Do you want to eat some of Daddy's cookies?" one of the girls continued.

"That's Pippa," Eric said. "Without the rain gear, you'll be able to tell her from Paige because Pippa has brown eyes like me, and Paige has hazel eyes like her mother. Other than that, they're identical."

"And I'm taller," the one Dinah believed was Paige said. "By half an inch."

"Only when you're standing on your tiptoes," Pippa argued.

"Do not," Paige protested.

"Do, too," Pippa countered.

"And so goes the Ramsey family," Eric said, laughing. "Oh, and, Dinah. I'd like you to meet my *sister*, Janice Laughlin. The girls and I live with her, and she watches them when I'm working."

Eric lived with his sister? Suddenly the heat of embarrassment began its creep from her neck, up her throat, to her cheeks. "Hello," she said, almost choking over the single word.

"But Daddy's going to get us a great big house of our own soon, where we can have a dog and…" Paige started.

"A cat," Pippa finished.

Dinah chanced a glance at Eric, whose expression was an odd one, caught between pain and amusement. He wanted to laugh, or cry. She couldn't tell which. And she wasn't sure she wanted to know. "Look, it's nice to meet all of you…Janice, Paige, Pippa. But I've really got to go and find my sister."

"Can we go see the baby?" Pippa cried. "Please?"

"Pretty please?" Paige joined in.

"Not right now," Eric said, trying to take a firm hand. "He's not feeling very well. But maybe in a few days."

But Eric wasn't very good at that firm hand, and it showed. Even to a casual observer such as herself, Dinah saw that he was just plain gooey when it came to his little girls. They had him wrapped around their little fingers, and he enjoyed every bit of it. He would be a very indulgent father, Dinah decided. And a very good one. Something also told her that Eric wasn't a man cheating on his wife. He was a man getting over something painful, for which she felt very bad. So bad, in fact, that she turned away without saying another word, and practically ran into the room where Angela was sitting, waiting for Gabby to return from seeing her baby. "Tell me about Eric," she whispered to Angela.

"What do you want to know?"

"Is he married?"

CHAPTER THREE

"WHY, I do believe you're flustered, Dinah." A smile crept to Angela's face as Dinah paced back and forth in the tiny hospital waiting room. "He is handsome, though, isn't he? Nice man. Smart. Good doctor, too."

"But is he married?"

"Oh, my… I guess you wouldn't know, would you?"

"Know what?"

"That he's a widower. I don't know the circumstances, except that it happened a long time ago, before he moved to White Elk."

Horror heaped on humiliation. She'd kissed him then accused him of something terrible. "He wears a wedding ring."

Her sister raised an inquisitive eyebrow. "I guess it's hard for him to let go. Is there something you want to tell me, Dinah?"

She shook her head, too upset to speak. From the moment he'd run into her on the road until now, nothing had been right between them except, perhaps, the way they'd worked together. Admittedly, that had been brilliant. A perfect medical union. Rare, especially for two strangers.

The kiss had been perfect, too. More perfect than she'd known a kiss could be. But she couldn't tell her sister because that kiss had been a huge mistake. Had meant nothing. After all, she'd been kissed before, and no kiss in her life had ever meant a thing. So, why should this one?

"Well, for what it's worth," Angela said, breaking into Dinah's thoughts, "I've hardly ever seen him come up to Pine Ridge, so once you're settled in there, and working, you probably won't run into him again. *If that's what you want.* At least, until I have my baby and you have to come to the hospital and visit me. And maybe you can work that out so you won't be here when he is." She laughed, and a wide grin spread over her face. "Unless you want to be where he is."

"I'm not interested," Dinah insisted.

"I didn't say you were."

"But that's what you were thinking."

"What I was thinking was that you're a little too…" She faked a frown, pretended to think. "What's the word I'm looking for? Is it…preoccupied? You're a little too preoccupied by the man. Or obsessed."

"Am not!" Dinah argued as yet another good, firm, and very telling blush spread over her cheeks on account of Eric.

"Whatever you say."

"I say I'm not preoccupied. And I'm not obsessed, either."

"Whatever you say."

"I said I'm not!" Dinah protested again, yet the heat kept rising in her, along with the timbre of her voice. OK, so she'd never been a very good liar. As a child, that little trait had been the bane of her existence, like when she'd tried to explain away the missing candy from the bowl on her grandmother's coffee table, or when she'd been late to school. "And I don't want to talk about it anymore." Even though, avoidance was a good plan. If she avoided Eric, there would be no more hostilities, no more humiliation. No more kisses. The problem was, she wanted to see him. Bad problem. Bad, *bad* problem. Because she didn't know why. Which caused the heat in her cheeks to positively flame.

What the hell had that been about? Eric kicked the trash can next to his desk, knocking it over, spilling out the paper contents. It had been about a kiss, that's what. And now he felt as guilty as hell. Sure, he was a red-blooded man. He hadn't been without certain desires all this time. But desiring and acting on those desires were two different things, and he wasn't ready to act on them. Had never come close to acting on them, and suddenly, that was the only thing on his mind.

Five years was a long time—a lifetime of feeling married yet not having his wife here. But that's what his life had turned into. And he didn't regret it, because he truly wasn't ready to change things. The girls needed their mother's memory kept alive, and he was the only one who could do that. They were so young, and all they knew were the things he told them, so how could it be time to move past that point?

Swallowing hard, Eric looked at Patricia's

picture on his desk. God, he missed her. His friends, even Janice kept telling him it was time to get on with his life, but he didn't feel like it was time. He was waiting for…well, he wasn't sure. Maybe a sign? Or, a push?

But not a kiss. That had been a mistake. Still, it had been a nice kiss, one that had reaffirmed the fact that he still had passions, albeit buried pretty deeply. Big mistake, though, because the feelings that had come immediately after… Then practically being accused of cheating on his wife when, in fact, that's exactly what he felt like, pounded him hard. He hadn't kissed a woman other than Patricia for ten years. Hadn't ever wanted to. So what was it about Dinah that had caused that to happen? And make no mistake, he'd been the one to step up to her and pull her into his arms. His initiative, his kiss.

He felt like hell for it. Pure hell.

What's more, he didn't trust himself not to do it again.

Bending down, he righted the trash can, then stood back up and studied it for a moment. Then kicked it again.

* * *

"You're stirring that sauce like a woman possessed."

Dinah spun away from the stove and almost bumped into Eric. She'd thought about him a thousand times these past few days, thought about the kiss, too, and would have called him, ostensibly to check on Bryce, even though she'd been kept up to date with the baby's progress via her sister. Which left her no reason to call Eric and stir things up between them again, except she did want to apologize for what she'd said. She'd even considered driving down to White Elk to set things straight with him. But how could she face him when she'd practically accused him of being a liar and a cheat?

Avoidance was easier, she decided. She and Eric didn't have any kind of relationship going, they owed each other nothing, had no expectations. So, for her, this was the best thing to do. She was good at it, had had a lifetime of practice. "You're not supposed to be in the kitchen. Didn't you see the sign on the door?"

"I did." He stepped a little closer, looking into the saucier on the stovetop. "Hollandaise sauce?"

"Bordelaise. And you can't be in here, looking at my Bordelaise."

"Actually, I can. I'm one of the on-call county health inspectors. It gets me into pretty much any place I want to go. Including your kitchen."

His brown eyes twinkled so brightly she had to avert her eyes, stare at loaves of bread she'd pulled out of the oven just a while ago. "So this is an inspection?" Whirling back to the stove, she returned her wobbly attention to the thickening sauce, trying to ignore the fact that he was standing so close to her. "Aren't you supposed to notify us when you're going to do that?"

"No. That defeats the purpose of trying to find infractions. If you know I'm coming, you hide things."

She picked up a long-handled spoon and began to stir, only to find that her sauce was already sticking to the bottom of the saucier. Curdled beyond repair and sticking to the pan. He had been there less than two minutes and she'd managed to ruin the Bordelaise, so what was it about Eric Ramsey that did that to her? The high humiliation factor? Because she certainly seemed to humiliate herself every time she was near him. "So, inspect. Help yourself. Check the pantry, the cold storage. And don't forget the freezer. Or the grease traps." She set aside the ruined sauce, and decided not to start over until he was gone. Bordelaise could be delicate and she didn't want to mess up another one.

"You can't use that, can you?" he asked pointing to the saucier. "Any way to resurrect it?"

"Is insulting my culinary skills part of your duty as inspector?" she snapped. Why didn't he leave? Why did he make her hands shake?

She looked down at her trembling hands, and jammed them into to her pants pockets before he noticed.

"Your cooking skills looked pretty good. Not as good as your nursing skills, though."

"Former nursing skills," she insisted, feeling the bite of nostalgia already.

"Well, whatever you're calling yourself these days, I wanted to tell you that Bryce was sent up to Salt Lake City, he's had his second surgery, and he's doing fine. Came through beautifully."

"You could have phoned."

"I could have, but then I wouldn't have been able to give you these."

He jiggled a bag. She heard the paper crinkle, but she wasn't sensing what could be in the bag, and it was quite clear that he wasn't about to tell her. In other words, it was her move. If she wanted to find out, she'd have to turn around and look...look at what was in the bag. Look at him. Look into his eyes. "What?" she asked, without giving in.

"These." He jiggled the bag again, teasing her.

OK, so now her interest was piqued. She turned. Studied the brown bag for a moment. Thrust out her hand to take it. Inside were six cookies, chocolate chip. Misshapen, a little overdone. And quite obviously a gift from his daughters. "You've taken up baking?" she asked, trying to sound disinterested as she pulled out a cookie and headed straight to the fridge for milk.

"The only thing I bake is a frozen dinner, in the microwave, and technically I don't think that's even considered baking, is it?"

Dinah poured two mugs of milk and handed one to Eric. "Chocolate-chip cookies always have to have milk."

"Do you dunk?" he asked.

"Of course I dunk! Is there any other way to eat a chocolate-chip cookie?"

Eric pulled a cookie from the bag and was the first one to dunk. Dinah followed suit, took a bite, and swallowed. Politely. Trying not to make the face Eric was making. "They lack a little in refinement," he said. "But they're getting better."

At five, she and Angela had been baking cookies like pros. With help from their mother, of course. But Pippa and Paige didn't have a mother, and suddenly, she felt sad for them, sad for the things Eric's little girls were missing. Dinah knew how it felt having a parent missing from her life, but her parent had left by choice. He hadn't wanted daughters, or a woman capable of giving him only daughters. Pippa and Paige's situation was so different, so tragic. "Maybe I could give them a lesson or two. If you don't mind?" The offer was genuine, although she didn't know where it had come from. Dinah instantly regretted it because helping the girls would keep her in closer contact with Eric. That was something she didn't want, and could ill afford.

"You'd do that? Teach the girls to cook? Janice has been supervising them in the kitchen, but her skills are, well, not much better than theirs. But

if you could spend a little time with the girls…"
He dunked his cookie, and studied it for a
moment. "They love cooking, and doing so many
of the little-girl things I can't do with them. So,
if you really want to do this, I'd appreciate it,
because I've got a lot of years ahead of me, eating
these things." He popped the last of his cookie
into his mouth and washed it down with the milk.
Big gulps of milk.

They agreed that the following afternoon
would be good for the first cookie lesson then
Dinah returned to her dinner preparation. But
Eric didn't leave right away. He simply stood
back, watching her, which made her nervous.
Finally, after she fumbled her way through
adding too much vinegar to a vinaigrette then
having to compensate for her mistake, she con-
fronted him. "Look, Eric. You can't stay here. If
you're going to inspect the kitchen, or any part
of the restaurant, do it. If not, please leave. I'm
not a very organized cook yet, as you can tell, and
you're distracting me. And I've got to get dinner
service up and going within the next hour."

"I had dinner here last night. You're pretty good."

"You did?" That surprised her. But she never

looked into the dining room, so she wouldn't have known.

"I was curious to see how you were doing. Janice and my niece, Debbi, took the girls out for pizza and a movie. I had an evening off. So I decided to come and see for myself."

"And?"

"It was good. Better than that thing I was going to throw into the microwave."

Dinah laughed. "That's high praise, coming from an obvious gastronome such as yourself."

"OK, so I'd just as soon eat a cheese sandwich as the Filet Oscar I had last night. Over the years, I've gotten used to less-than-polished meals. But as meals go, I'd say yours was pretty polished. In fact, I might eat here again some time. Might even ask you to come and be a nurse in my trauma department again some time. Our nurse practitioner, Fallon O'Gara, is going away on a short holiday, and I thought…"

"You thought wrong!" she snapped, spinning away from him and heading straight into the walk-in pantry. Once inside, she felt like closing the door behind her and turning off the light. Maybe that would make him go away. Or maybe all the bad thoughts would disappear in the dark, vanish into some little black crevice and never return.

"Dinah!" he called through the door.

"I'm busy!" she yelled back. It hurt, and she knew it showed. She didn't want him to see, didn't want him to know that one little kiss had turned her already-confused situation into more confusion than she was able to deal with. "Please, just let me do my work."

He opened the door, but didn't enter. Didn't turn on the light either. "Why did you leave nursing, Dinah? What happened? Because I took the liberty of checking your credentials, and—"

"You what?" she sputtered, flying out of the pantry and slamming the pouches of gravy starter she'd grabbed from a shelf down on the counter. "How…how could you do that?"

"I was curious. You're too insistent that you don't want to be a nurse, yet you're so passionate about it. Since I had every intention of offering you a temporary job, I checked."

"Well, good for you. Now you know." And she wanted to crawl off somewhere and be alone.

"I was told that you were competent. Competent,

that's all. Which doesn't make any sense, because I saw you work. Saw how good you are."

"It's none of your business!" she snapped.

"It became my business when you stepped into my operating room to assist me."

"Which wasn't exactly my choice, if you recall. You were the one who wanted me there."

"And I don't regret that because I saw what you can do. Saw your passion. Which is why I don't understand what I was told."

"Well, believe it. It's true. I was competent. That's all there is to say, except I'm not looking for a nursing job. So you can leave now." She marched over to the hanging rack above the center prep island, grabbed a large copper pot down off its hook and slammed it down on the stove top. When it didn't slam hard enough to satisfy her, Dinah picked up the pan and slammed it again, harder this time. "What gives you the right?" she cried, spinning to face him. "I came here to cook, and to be left alone. Not to have someone like you dig into my past."

"Your past doesn't reconcile with what I saw."

"And it doesn't have to. I quit nursing. Walked away from it, and that's the end of the story. If you still want me to give your girls cooking lessons, I'll do that. But after that you have to leave me alone. That's the deal, Eric. Take it or leave it. I'll help your girls, but that's as far as we go." She brushed past Eric and went to the cold storage, where she grabbed six large onions, bundled them into her apron, and marched straight back to the prep area. "And you don't get to ask questions. That's also part of this deal."

"Then I have to accept it, don't I?"

"Do you?" Rather than waiting for an answer, Dinah set about the chore of prepping onions. Peeling off skins, cutting off both ends, she lit into them, fast and furious, alternately swiping at the onion tears with the back of the sleeve of her chef's jacket and chopping like a woman possessed.

"Look, Dinah, it was only a kiss. OK? People do it all the time and it doesn't usually mean anything."

She chopped even faster, the sound of her knife striking the cutting board and never breaking rhythm.

"I apologize for it, and that's all I can say. I'm sorry we did it, sorry I upset you."

The speed of her chopping picked up even

more. In fact, she was whooshing through her little pile of onions so fast it surprised her.

"But I'd like us to get past that, and be friends. For my girls' sakes. Can we do that?" Her knife slipped. She whacked her finger, and blood immediately spilled out onto her cutting surface.

Dinah dropped her knife and jumped back, not reacting from pain because she didn't yet feel the pain. But the sight of blood on the butcher block… "I was a damned good nurse," she whispered, taking the kitchen towel Eric held out to her. "Better than competent."

"I know that. So, let me take a look at your finger," he said, taking hold of her hand.

But she pulled back from him. "It's a nick. I'm fine. Just…just leave me alone." Hurrying over to the sink, she ran cold water over her wound, and once the blood was washed away, she assessed the severity.

"You're right," he said, taking his place at her side. "It's only a nick. You'll be fine." He pulled a bandage from the kitchen first-aid kit and wrapped it around her cut, his fingers so gentle on her she shivered. "You OK?" he asked, when the gooseflesh rose on her arms.

"I'm busy, and this is taking up too much time."
She slid her hand from his grasp and fought hard
not to shiver again as her flesh slid across his.
Even so, the goosebumps remained.

"So, what happened, Dinah?"

"The knife slipped."

"You know what I mean."

She did. He wanted to know things she didn't
talk about. Deep, hurtful things. But she could
make it simple, make it impersonal, then he'd go
away. "I was engaged to a man who thought I
was better suited to the kitchen than the
hospital." She held up her finger. "And as you
can see, I'm not that well suited to the kitchen.
But I promise to keep the knives away from your
girls if you still want me to teach them."

"Why do I get the feeling that you're making
light of something that's not light at all?"

"It's complicated. And not very interesting.
And if you agree to the cooking lessons then
you drop this. You don't talk about it, don't ask
questions, don't express an opinion. It's over,
I've moved on, and that includes to the kitchen,
not the hospital. That's the deal, the only deal."

"One opinion, then consider it dropped. I want

you to know that *I know* you're a talented nurse. One of the best I've ever seen. If it's the kitchen you want, that's fine, but that man who was supposed to love you enough to marry you was wrong. Now, no more opinions. I want you to teach my daughters how to bake."

It was a deal that left a bitter taste, apparently for both of them because the memories of that betrayal hurt Dinah, and because Eric wanted to know more. Much more. But couldn't ask. This was how it had to be, though. Dinah was reconciled to that because her history repeated itself and, for once, she was fighting hard not to let that happen again. Eric tempted her, and she caught herself wanting to be tempted. But she couldn't let herself be. It was as simple as that. Or as difficult.

Yet one glance into Eric Ramsey's eyes and she wondered if she could do what had to be done. Because he stirred things inside her she'd never known could be stirred.

"I thought you'd be at the hospital." At least, Dinah had hoped he'd be there, which didn't turn out to be the case because he was standing in the doorway, looking drop-dead gorgeous in his jeans and black T-shirt. A distraction like that was something she didn't need and, for a moment, she considered cancelling the cookie lesson, or postponing it until he was gone. But while she struggled against taking a second lip-licking look at Eric, a whirlwind from behind literally pitched him forward, almost into her arms—a giggling, squealing whirlwind of little girls, which jolted her back into the moment, and into the recognition that this was not about her, or Eric. She'd made a promise to Pippa and Paige, and she couldn't break it.

"Sorry about that," he said, shoving off her and trying to stand upright against the twin force jumping up and down behind his back. "They've been excited about this all morning. I couldn't calm them down."

Pippa and Paige each wore a tiny version of a chef's apron. If it weren't for the fact that the aprons were embroidered with their names, she wouldn't have been able to tell the girls apart, they looked so much alike. Pippa had the brown eyes, she remembered, while Paige had the hazel—if they stood still long enough to get a good look. Which wasn't the case right now.

Pretty girls. Exuberant. They looked like Eric, with dark hair and beautiful, perfect smiles.

"We have lots of chocolate chips, if Paige didn't eat them all," Pippa said.

"Did not," Paige defended.

"Saw you," Pippa argued.

"Saw *you*," Page retorted.

"Which is why you should always buy twice as many chocolate chips as the recipe calls for," Dinah interrupted, stepping around Eric and entering the house. Nice house. Homey. But it didn't suit Eric. Of course, it wasn't Eric's house. He lived with his sister. "That way, you'll have enough for your cookies, and enough for your tummies."

The girls each latched on to one of Dinah's hands, and pulled her toward the kitchen in a collective effort. "We got everything ready last night," Pippa said. "And checked it again this morning to make sure nobody took anything." She gave her sister a dubious look, one which was returned.

"Good luck," Eric said from the doorway. He was standing there, filling up the frame, arms folded casually across his chest. Smiling.

"I think we'll manage quite nicely," she

replied, wishing he'd go away. She didn't want him there, didn't want to keep looking to see what he was watching, afraid that he was watching her, afraid that he wasn't. "Am I going to teach you how to bake cookies, too?" Hopefully he'd take the hint and leave.

"On call all night, on duty all morning. Meaning nap time for me."

He did look tired. But it was a long-time weariness she saw more than anything else, and her heart went out to him. His life couldn't be easy. Between his work and his girls she doubted Eric had any time left over for himself. "We'll save some cookies for you," she promised, then turned away. Her thoughts were too cozy, she had no business sympathizing with the man. Had no business having any kind of thoughts about him.

As she began to hunt for the proper bowls, Eric motioned Paige and Pippa over to him. "Girls, Daddy's going to sleep for a little while. Be good for Dinah. Do what she tells you to do, and come get me when the last batch comes out of the oven because I like my cookies warm." With that, he kissed each one on the top of her head, then plodded down the hall. Seconds later, the distinct thud of a shutting door told Dinah she could relax. Suddenly, though, it was just her and two eager, ricocheting little girls. Sick children she knew how to deal with. But these girls…

It probably wasn't the nicest thing for him to do, leaving her in the kitchen with the girls. They were high energy on a normal day and this wasn't a normal day for them. But he couldn't be there. Couldn't watch the cozy scene going on. Back in the days when Patricia had been pregnant with the twins, she'd had so many plans, so many hopes and dreams for her family. And sometimes the cruel bite of how unfair life was simply got to him. Today was one of those days. It should have been Patricia teaching her girls to cook, Patricia and the girls in *their* kitchen, not in his sister's. Seeing Dinah in there, doing something that should have been Patricia's to do, tore at his heart, and it had nothing to do with Dinah. She was just being nice.

But, damn it, the girls were all over her, so happy to be involved in such a simple thing. When Dinah had volunteered to do this, it had sounded like a good idea. But now the reality of it made him question why he'd wanted to bring Dinah closer to their lives. The girls had a hard enough time hanging on to a mother they'd never known, and this wasn't going to make his task of keeping Patricia in their lives any easier. But something was nagging at him to move on with his life. It had been for a while, and Dinah only accentuated it.

Just look at him! An adult with children, living in his sister's home, making do. Postponing life. Refusing to move forward.

Back in California, before he'd agreed to come to White Elk, he'd had his mother to help him. She'd swooped in to take care of the girls, and promised to stay as long as he needed her. Which had turned out to be until the time he'd moved to White Elk and allowed his sister to do the same thing. He'd taken an apartment here, hired a nanny for his daughters, planning on putting life on a permanent delay. Janice had come here, with his niece shortly after, solely to help him, once it had become clear he was struggling to manage without family. Once she'd got here, she'd found a real life right away. She'd bought a house, established a business, made friends everywhere.

On the other hand, he'd moved in with her, at her request, to make her care of the twins more convenient, while he'd secluded himself at the hospital. His life on an even bigger delay.

That's exactly what it was, and most of the time he didn't think about that because it worked well enough. The girls were happy, they didn't feel the pressures. Right now, though, with Dinah assuming a mother's duty… "Damn," he muttered, dropping onto his bed. A single bed. For one. Grown men didn't sleep in single beds, and this was just another reminder of how he'd allowed things to get out of hand. It was his duty to make sure his daughters came first in his life, but what came after them? What was out there for him?

"It's not easy, Patricia," he whispered, looking at the wedding ring on his finger. For a few moments he simply stared at the glint of the gold and the plain contours of it, trying to empty his mind of everything. Yet for once his mind wouldn't empty. It was chock full of memories… good ones like the day he'd met Patricia, the evening he'd proposed marriage, the afternoon they'd married. Flashes of the day she'd learnt she was pregnant were there, the excitement of discovering it was going to be twins…hopes, dreams, futures to plan. But the bad memories were there, too…her obstetrician telling him she'd bled out during the delivery, that she was in a critical condition. Sitting at her bedside, never leaving for three days, never letting go of her hand. Never having the chance to tell her that her daughters were beautiful and healthy…

Eric swiped at the tear straying down his cheek. The kitchen. The damned kitchen is what caused this…what *forced* this. It was time.

He stroked the gold band on his finger, twisted it around, stroked it again. It *was* time. He resisted it, tried to argue himself out of it. Didn't want it. Dear God, he didn't want it. But it had to be time. He needed a life, too. Needed to be normal again. For himself. Especially for Pippa and Paige.

On a deep, sad sigh Eric slipped the wedding band off his finger, kissed it and held it to his heart for a while. He wasn't sure how long. But eventually he stood, walked over to the dresser and opened the top drawer. There, nestled into the corner, was a small velvet box with another plain gold band. A smaller one. The one he'd placed on Patricia's finger nearly seven years ago, promising her he'd buy her something more beautiful someday. She'd laughed at him, called him silly, told him the plain gold band was all she wanted, that to her it was the most beautiful ring in the world.

It was another few moments before he placed his gold band with hers then, reluctantly, shut the box lid and tucked the box away.

Someday, when the girls were a little older, he would have both rings melted down and made into heart pendants for them. That's why he'd kept Patricia's ring. He'd wanted Pippa and Paige to have it, to have something that had been so loved by her. Now it only seemed right that they would have both rings...rings that belonged together, for ever.

Yes, that was a good idea. And it did give him some comfort as he stared at the empty, stark white band of skin on his finger. Then, for the next few minutes, he leaned against the bedroom door and listened to the laughter coming from the kitchen. It was good, he thought. Bad in so many ways, painful beyond anything he could have expected, but good, too. But, damn, it hurt.

Good, bad, or otherwise, first thing tomorrow he

was going to start looking for a house for one dad and two daughters. Yes, it was time for that, too.

Funny, though, how he'd only now come to terms with that after he'd met Dinah. It had nothing to do with her, of course, but the timing was…odd. Unexpected. "One thing at a time," he whispered, plodding into the bathroom to splash cold water on his face. Taking off a wedding ring didn't mean he was going to go out and get involved right away. It was only a first step. Truth was, the second step scared him to death. Especially if it was in the direction of someone who came with so much baggage. And Dinah did have her fair share of it. Yes, one thing at a time, and that didn't include the beautiful nurse-chef-amazing woman who was in the kitchen, teaching his girls how to bake chocolate-chip cookies.

Or did it?

CHAPTER FOUR

"No, THE chocolate chips go in after the flour."
Pippa had chocolate smeared all over her face.
Paige, on the other hand, had wiped it on her
apron. And Dinah was loving every minute of
this. In fact, she couldn't remember when she'd
had so much fun. It was like everything was right
in their world, and their world was all there was.
She was drawn into it, and happy to be there.

"But won't the flour turn them all white?"
Pippa asked. "Maybe if we put them in first, then
cover them up…"

"With more chocolate chips," Paige chimed in.
"If we put more chocolate chips on top of the
first ones, then the first ones won't get all white
from the flour."

"Then how do you keep the ones on top from
getting white?" Pippa asked, somewhat miffed.

"It comes off," Dinah said, trying to hold back her laugh. These little girls were deadly serious about this. They wanted to make perfect cookies, and she wondered if they strove for such perfection in everything they did. It was so cute, and she owed Eric a great big thank-you for letting her do this. "Once we get everything all mixed together, and get the cookies in the oven, everything will come right off the chocolate chips."

Both girls frowned at her, like they didn't believe her. "But Aunt Janice makes us go to another room so she can have room to wipe the chocolate chips clean," Paige said in all earnestness.

Probably because by this time in the process Janice was tired of answering all the questions and wanted to get on with it. By last count, each girl had asked Dinah about a hundred, only she'd thought it was fun trying to find answers for questions she would have never, in her life, anticipated. *Where does salt come from? Who was the first person to ever cook food and how did they know they were cooking if cooking hadn't been invented yet? Wouldn't it be better to have a whole bunch of aprons in different colors to match all the foods so they wouldn't look dirty when food gets spilled on them?*

Maybe for Janice the questions got tiring, but for Dinah they were amazing. She liked the challenge. Liked the way the girls thought. But she was concerned that they were trying to be much older than they were and, in effect, losing a little of their childhood. Maybe because their care was, by necessity, left up to so many people? Or maybe because their father wasn't at a place in his life where he knew how to have fun anymore, and the girls mimicked what they saw. "Well, I'm sure Aunt Janice is used to doing it her way, but this way has always worked for me."

The girls looked at each other, considering something unspoken between them—that twin connection—then both came up smiling. "Can I mix?" Pippa asked.

"Me, too?" Page also asked.

"I have two bowls, so I'd say I'm going to need two good mixers." Ten minutes later, with all the ingredients split evenly between the bowls, and mixed as well as any cookie dough had ever been mixed, it was time to get the dough to the cookie pan.

"Let me warn you that this is where they eat more than they bake."

Dinah spun around, almost knocking into Eric, who had crept back to the kitchen and was leaning against the fridge, watching. Barefoot, hair mussed, shirt untucked…wickedly sexy. "Do you always sneak up on people that way?" Her voice was amazingly calm considering how nothing else about her was.

"Only people worth sneaking up on," he said, stepping aside as Dinah brushed herself against him, trying to wedge herself between the fridge and the utility drawer.

"Why aren't you sleeping, Daddy?" Paige asked.

"I discovered I wasn't sleepy. And I thought I would come out here and wait for my cookies."

"Then wait in the dining room," Dinah said, brushing up against him one more time on her way back from the utility drawer. It caused a chill to shoot up her spine, first time, this time. A chill she was fighting to ignore. Why was it that whatever governed one person's attraction to another was working overtime with her right now? She'd never been this wildly attracted to Charles. Hadn't gotten chills *ever* during her brief marriage to Damien. But Eric… It's because she couldn't, that's why! Couldn't have him, couldn't get involved. Couldn't even think about it. Couldn't! And that little streak of opposition in her that knew she *couldn't* was rebelling. Hence the attraction, and the shivers. It was simply a personal little insurrection.

Good explanation, she decided as she handed large spoons to each of the girls. She turned back to insist that Eric step away, but surprisingly he already had. He hadn't gone all the way to the dining room, but he was in the doorway, and the look on his face… It was distant. He was staring out the back window, but if she'd had a paycheck coming in, she'd bet every penny of it he wasn't seeing anything outside.

"How much?" one of the girls said insistently.

"What?" she asked.

"How much cookie dough?"

Pippa had a chunk on her spoon that approximated the amount for six cookies, which snapped Dinah back into the baking lesson. "Not quite that much," she instructed, showing the girls the proper amount. Then she showed them the appropriate spacing of the dough on the pan, and stepped away while they worked to get the unbaked cookies lined up in perfect little rows. Once, when they were halfway through, she looked back at Eric, who was still there. Physically. But his eyes were still so distant.

Propped there against the doorframe, he looked…sad. She studied him for a moment, trying not to be obvious. But something caught her eye. Something missing. So, when had he removed his wedding ring? "No, Paige. You can't squeeze them that close together. They have to have room to expand, so spread them out a little more. Just look at the first row I did, and copy that."

The girls chattered away as they finished putting the dough on the pan, while Dinah supervised. Then, as Dinah, not the girls, placed the cookies in the oven, Eric withdrew from the kitchen altogether. She thought about going after him, asking him if there was anything she could do to help, but her two little assistant cooks weren't about to budge from the kitchen while the timer was counting down the minutes, and she wasn't going to leave them alone in there. So she sat down at the kitchen table and fielded another battery of questions from the girls.

"Who was the one who decided how long a minute was?" Pippa asked.

"And how did he know it was a minute and not an hour, if no one had ever had a minute before?" Paige chimed in.

"The girls are great," Dinah said. She sat a plate of warm cookies on the table on the patio outside. Eric was leaning against the deck rail outside in the backyard, this time looking into the kitchen through the window. "You've done an amazing job with them. And if you don't mind, they want me to take them shopping for…well, let's just say, five-year-old unmentionables."

"Unmentionables?" He arched his eyebrows, even though the eyes underneath them were still distracted.

"Well, panties. Apparently Aunt Janice buys boring panties and your daughters want…"

Eric blinked himself back into the conversation. "They want new panties? You don't have to," he said.

"But I don't mind. And I sort of promised them manicures and hair appointments."

"Manicures? They're five!"

Dinah laughed. "But a girl is never too young to have her hair and fingernails done." Her eyes wanted to trail down to his ring finger, but she resisted. "And Pippa and Paige informed me they've never had a manicure. So…"

"They're growing up." He sighed heavily.

"A little bit."

"And I don't have a clue."

"Well, that's probably true. But it's curable, because I have an idea your daughters will always let you know exactly what they need, and when. Like I said, they're amazing little girls. Full of life."

"Like their mother." He cleared his throat and continued. "The girls and I…we're going to move," he said, out of the blue. "I love my sister, but she's put up with us for too long, without ever complaining. She disrupted her life back in California and moved here with us because she didn't want us coming here alone. But she's the one who got her life together, not me. And I think it's time the girls and I had a place of our own so she can live more of that life."

He was moving out? Did that mean he was starting to move on? Eventually, it always happened. Her mother had, after a while. She herself had, after her divorce from Damien, and in a sense this was part of her moving on from Charles. But Eric's situation was something she couldn't even begin to understand. "You're sure you're ready for this?" she asked, for a lack of something better to say. "I mean, I know that you have to get to a certain point where it feels right, feels like it's time. When Damien and I were married—"

"You were married?" he interrupted.

"Not for long. I was barely in my twenties. Not so smart about relationships. He was…not who I thought he was. The marriage lasted for less than a year, but I stayed near him for a year longer than that because I couldn't force myself to make the move. You know, move on. I suppose I always hoped something would change, that the situation wasn't really what it was. So I left him, reconciled, left, reconciled…"

"And?"

"I wised up when I finally realized that you don't change a cheating husband, no matter what he promises you. No matter how much you want things to be different, some things will never change."

"I'm sorry," he said, rubbing the empty spot on his ring finger. "That had to be rough."

"It was." Because she'd grown up picturing herself living happily-ever-after. Because she'd grown up wanting it. Sadly, she didn't believe in that anymore. "Moving on wasn't easy."

"I know," he said. "Not easy, but necessary. But I've put it off too long, so now…"

"Can we bake some more?" Paige called from the door. "We got them ready on the pan."

"Duty calls," Dinah said, backing away from Eric. "And it's pretty demanding."

"I appreciate this, Dinah. I know we've got a little friction going between us, and I'm sorry about that." He chuckled. "Seems like I'm always apologizing for something, doesn't it? But I do appreciate what you're doing for my girls. And if they need some new *unmentionables* and a manicure, and you don't mind…"

"I don't mind, Eric. In fact, I'm looking forward to it." She glanced down at his empty finger this time, and this time he saw her do it. But he didn't say anything.

"Eric, I'm so sorry," she whispered, laying her

hand on his as Pippa ran up, grabbed her by the other hand and started tugging.

"So am I. But it was time."

The broken whisper of his voice broke her heart as her hand slid away from his.

"Pedicures, too?" Eric said, smiling.

"A girl can't really have the full manicure experience without having the pedicure, too." It had been a wonderful morning, and she almost hated turning the girls over to their cousin, Debbi. But the arrangement had been made, and now she had the rest of the day ahead of her with nothing to do as it was her day off. Angela was simply too pregnant to do anything but sit with her feet up and manage the kitchen from that position, so Dinah had a lot of empty hours ahead of her. "I promised them we'd do it again some time. And have high tea in the lodge conservatory. Father permitting, of course."

"You're kidding, aren't you?"

Smile bright, eyes wide, she shrugged. "Actually, no. We all thought it was a brilliant idea."

Eric laughed out loud. "You know they're

taking advantage of you, don't you? They're very good at it. Better than I thought, apparently."

"You're probably right. But I'm a willing participant." Besides, she truly enjoyed their company, probably more than she'd thought she would. It was nice, being in the company of children who weren't sick. Although the more she was with the girls, the more she ached to get back to nursing. "I was wondering…would you need someone part-time in the hospital? Maybe the emergency department? I know you mentioned something the other day about nursing, but I thought maybe I could do something as a volunteer." Perhaps being back in a non-medical capacity would help ease the ache. "I could be a clerk, maybe check supplies…"

"Or be a nurse, like I suggested."

She shook her head adamantly. "I told you…"

"No, you didn't. But I agreed not to ask, so I won't. However, I still need a part-time *nurse*, and it's a serious offer."

Nursing scared her, though. In little bits and pieces she was OK. But how could she tell him that she no longer trusted herself for anything more than the bits and pieces? That all those words about being a good nurse were only words? That when she'd most needed to be professional in her duty, she'd let herself down? "Just forget it, OK? It was stupid of me to ask. I don't need to be back in a hospital. In fact, I don't want to be back in a hospital."

"Yes, you do. Or you wouldn't have asked. Wouldn't have come here to the hospital, to my emergency room, to tell me that you'd left the girls with my niece when that was the plan all along, and I knew you'd do that. Or you could have called and told me. But you didn't. Instead, you came here, which makes me think you want to come back. And don't tell me that we can't always have what we want, because I'm offering you the opportunity to have exactly what you want…a few hours a week in the emergency department. As a nurse, not as a clerk or someone who stocks the shelves." He stepped closer, leaned in to her. "I trust you here. I think you've lost your confidence for some reason I don't understand, and I'm not going to ask why, but I do trust you, Dinah."

"Well, maybe you shouldn't give away that trust so easily."

"And maybe *you* should trust my judgment, because I know a good nurse when I see one, and I'm looking at one right now."

She wanted to accept his offer. She *really* wanted to and, more than that, she was tempted. But he couldn't know how, in the waning moments of Molly's life, she'd lost part of herself. It was hard to explain, but it was like she was afraid to care now. The pain of it was unbearable, and to be around children was to care.

Tears welled up in her eyes, but she turned her head, blinked them back before Eric could see. "And maybe you should trust mine." Even the whisper of her voice was shattered by grief.

"Think about it. The offer will be here when you're ready."

"It's a tempting offer, and I appreciate it, but, no. I…don't think I should."

"When you're ready, Dinah. Like you told me the other day, it has to be when you're ready."

Eric stepped closer to her, so close she could feel the tickling of his warm breath on the back of her neck. So close she could smell the scent of soap on him. So close that if she turned around she'd be in his arms. Which was why she backed away, intent on leaving. She *did* want to be in his arms, feeling his comfort. Wanted it badly. Which was pure trouble.

"Can I help you with this?" he practically whispered. "I know I told you I'd let it go, but…"

"Promised. You *promised.*"

"And I'm not breaking my promise, Dinah. I *will* let it go, if that's what you want. But I want to help you, if I can. I don't know what's bothering you, but if you could trust me…"

If she could trust? Well, that was easier said than done, wasn't it? Dinah spun around, found herself so close to Eric it caught her off guard, and she swayed right into him. But pushed herself back immediately. "No, Eric. I can't trust. That's the problem. I can't, and I don't want to."

"Because of what your fiancé did to you?"

Dinah laughed bitterly. "Because I lost heart. Everything I thought I was, everything I thought I could be…I was wrong. Good skills don't necessarily make a good nurse, because a good nurse needs heart. When you lose it…"

"Or when it's broken?" he said gently.

"Or when you decide you don't have it." Emphatic words. Hard to say but she had to, if she were ever to believe them. Now maybe he would leave her alone. Pull back his offer and walk away. It was for the best, she told herself. Definitely for the best.

But Eric didn't so much as flinch. "Do you want to tell me what happened?"

"No." It still hurt too much. To fall so in love with a child with anencephaly made no sense to most people. A child born without a substantial part of her brain. A child with no prognosis for long-term survival. But that's exactly what she'd done.

"Then I'm sure you'll tell me when you can. And like I said, I did check your background, and there were no complaints. No reprimands. No mention of anything bad. So, unless I discover something different, or unless you tell me something that would make me change my mind about you—and I doubt that's going to happen—I'd like you working for a few hours on the night shift, if you decide to do this."

"Why?" she sputtered, disbelieving. How could he still want her? Or trust her?

"Because I believe in you. I'm not sure why you don't, but I have enough belief for the both of us. You're a good nurse, you belong in nursing and you'll see that once you're back. Maybe even find some of that heart you've lost. So, I'm offering a part-time, fill-in position, most likely only a part of a shift on the nights you'll work. But as a nurse, Dinah. Not a volunteer."

"Well, you're either a very brilliant man, Eric Ramsey, or a very stupid one." Dinah allowed a slight smile to touch her lips. "I haven't figured out which it is."

"Been called both. Maybe if you come work for me we can solve that puzzle together." He strolled to the door then stepped into the hall. But before he walked away, he turned back to Dinah. "And just so you know, the girls want to try their hand at oatmeal raisin cookies. And Pippa thinks she'll be up to a chocolate cake pretty soon."

"Thank you," she said, feeling the slightest bit of excitement. She wouldn't let herself get too excited, though, because that required some level of trust...trust in Eric. And as much as she wanted to, she couldn't. Wouldn't. Still, her stomach was starting to churn.

Five minutes later, on her way to the personnel office, what she'd just done finally began to sink in. She'd said yes to something she'd vowed not to do again. It was temporary position, and things would go right back to where they were in a matter of weeks, after Angela had delivered her baby and her help in White Elk was no longer needed. That's what she kept reminding herself on her way to fill out her employment papers. But that little warning voice was creeping in, too. *Not again, Dinah. Don't do this again.*

Wise words, but was she wise enough to listen to them? Because, with all her heart, she wanted to trust Eric.

Dinah's first official shift as a practicing nurse was quiet. In fact, if she hadn't been so keyed up to work as a nurse again, she could have had herself a very good nap because, except for one over-indulgent eater from the lodge and mild case of sniffles, she'd had the evening pretty much to herself. But that didn't matter. Nothing did, considering how she was back where she wanted to be, back where she belonged. So, for her six assigned hours, she patrolled the halls, tidied the supply cabinets, straightened the bed sheets, fluffed the pillows and simply existed in a place that made her happy. Dinah Corday, happy again. She desperately wished it could be permanent.

Eric called twice within the first hour, volunteering to come in if needed. But Dr. Jane McGinnis, on call for her shift, was sufficient for what seemed to be a very slow evening. In fact, she hid herself in a closed room and hung a "Do Not Disturb" sign on the door. Orthopedist by day, medical mystery novelist by night, Jane was in the middle of what she called revising a sagging middle, getting close to her deadline. Her orders were simply to leave her alone except for an emergency or unless she had the solution for getting the bound and gagged heroine out of the trunk of a car, safe and sound, while it was speeding at ninety miles per hour down the highway.

Since Dinah didn't have the solution to that one, she left Jane to her writing.

Then there was a grandmotherly-looking night clerk, Emoline Putters, on hand in the emergency department, spending her night transcribing doctors' notes, guzzling hot, black coffee and grumbling rather loudly, and often obscenely, over illegible handwriting. And Ed Lester, a man who mopped the halls and dusted the light fixtures, made his presence known a few times, pushing a broom up one corridor and down the next, but he did nothing more than nod and offer a half-salute to Dinah when she greeted him.

So, basically, Dinah was pretty much left alone.

At first she dreaded a long, empty night pacing up and down the hollow halls and listening to the squeak of her rubber soles on the tiled floor, and Emoline's muttering off in the distance, then at the halfway point of her shift she was amazed how quickly her first hours had flown by.

The hours, no matter how fast or slow, didn't matter, though. This was all about being back where she belonged. Smelling the smells, hearing the sounds. Home.

"Want me to go out and scare up some business?" Eric asked, as Dinah scurried by treatment room number three on her way to do nothing in particular.

She glanced in, saw him stretched out on the exam table, feet up, head propped up on several pillows, hands clasped behind his head. "Are you checking up on me?"

"Maybe."

She wasn't sure if she should be flattered or

angry. "If that's standard for all your new employees, fine. Check. But if it's something about me…"

"Don't be so defensive. Jane called. She's at a plot point she doesn't want interrupted unless we absolutely have to. She asked if I could back her up."

"A plot point."

"She's going to donate part of the proceeds from her book to expanding the orthopedic wing. We're in ski country here. We want that expansion, so we do what we have to."

"So we're not supposed to call the doctor on call."

"Not when she's at a crucial plot point." He swung his legs down off the exam table and sat straight up. "If we can at all avoid it."

"You run a very lenient hospital here, Doctor."

"We try to. I came from a very typical medical background, it worked. But when I got here, this just seemed like the place to…to be something different, do something different. We try to make our medicine more relaxed, more personal."

"More involved?"

He nodded. Neil and I both felt that medicine's moving too far away from being personal, which is why we decided to go in the opposite direction when we bought the hospital. We were both starting over at the time…he'd just gone through a messy divorce, I was recently widowed. Fresh starts all the way round."

"Easier said than done." She wanted a fresh start, but she hadn't yet figured how to rid herself of the stale past.

"Or easier done than said, if you want it badly enough. I wanted it and, thank God, I found White Elk."

"Then you're happy here?"

"We're all three happy here." Finally, he stood. "You could be, too, if—"

"Got one coming in," Emoline Putters' voice boomed over the intercom.

Eric chuckled. "What she lacks in finesse she makes up for in efficiency." As he headed out toward the hall, with Dinah practically right behind him, they greeted a frantic mother leading the way while her husband carried a child through the emergency door.

"He's not responding to us," the mother cried, while Eric took the boy in his arms and rushed into the first treatment room. "Barely able to talk."

"When did this start?" Dinah asked.

"About an hour ago. We heard him moaning…"

"Has he been sick?"

The father stepped in and slid his arm around his wife's waist. "My name is Frank Jackson, this is my wife, Elaine. Our son, Henry, is ten. He hasn't been sick, at least not that we've seen. And he hasn't said anything to us about not feeling well. But about an hour ago we heard him moaning, thought it was an upset stomach, but he wouldn't respond to us when we tried talking to him…just moaned."

Dinah squeezed Mrs Jackson's arm. "We'll let you know as soon as *we* know something." She turned and hurried into the treatment room and joined Eric at the side of the exam table.

"Blood pressure's normal, pulse rate fine, pupils equal, respirations perfect," Eric said.

"He wasn't sick prior to this episode." Instinctively, she picked up his wrist to take a pulse, felt the boy flinch. "Any temperature?"

Eric shook his head as he placed his stethoscope into his ears and bent to listen to Henry's lungs. "Sound clear," he finally said. "Heart sounds good, too."

"But he's not responding," Dinah said, staring across the table at Eric. "I wonder how his reflexes are. Could be serious, if he has The Drop."

"The Drop," Eric responded, nodding. Fighting back a smile. "Yes, very serious. Perhaps you should do that test, Nurse."

"Very well, Doctor." She picked up Henry's arm, held it steady for a moment then dropped it onto the table. There was a hesitation in movement, just for a split second, before his arm fell.

"Looks like a partial case of The Drop to me," Eric said.

Dinah glanced down at the boy, barely containing her own smile. "Thank heavens for that. Because the needle you have to use for a full case of The Drop is so big…" She held up her hands in front of Henry's face, indicating something at least the size of Eric's forearm.

Henry's face scrunched, but he still didn't respond.

"But I don't have a half-sized needle for a partial case of The Drop," Eric said.

"Then I think we can use a full-sized needle and stick it only halfway into him. Wouldn't that work?"

"Good idea, Nurse. Why don't you roll Henry over on his side and I'll get the injection ready."

"Are you going to give the shot in his bottom, Doctor?" Dinah asked.

Eric's grin was from ear to ear. "I know it will hurt worse there, but I think it's for the best. And since he's not awake, he won't feel it."

"Very well, Doctor." With that, Dinah started to roll Henry over on his side, but his eyes popped open.

"No!" he screamed. "I don't want a shot!"

"But you could get sick again," Dinah said, "and one shot should keep you from getting The Drop for at least a year."

Henry bolted upright on the exam table. "I'm not sick. I wasn't sick. I was just…"

"But you have all the symptoms," Eric said.

"I don't have symptoms," Henry protested. "I just didn't want to go to school tomorrow. We're having a math test, and I didn't…" Big tears rolled down his cheeks. "I didn't study for it. Am I in trouble?"

"Faking an illness and scaring your parents the way you did could be very serious," Dinah said.

"And what if someone who was really sick needed our help but we couldn't take care of them because we were taking care of you?" Eric stepped up to the table and helped Henry to the floor. "And it costs a lot of money to come to the emergency room. Are you going to be able to pay for this?"

"M-money?" he asked.

Dinah and Eric both nodded solemnly.

"I have an allowance…my lunch money."

Dinah slipped out into the hall to talk with the Jacksons while Eric continued the discussion with Henry, and by the time the Jackson family left the hospital, the arrangement was made that Henry would pay back what he owed for his little prank by volunteering every Saturday morning for the next several weeks. His duty would be as the toy monitor in the hospital waiting room's play area for children.

"You spotted that one pretty fast," Eric said, stretching back out on an exam table.

"Experience. He was peeking at us when he thought we weren't looking." She laughed. "The harder they scrunch their faces, the more they're faking."

"You've used The Drop before?"

"In some variation. Threaten them with the big needle, and they'll confess every time."

"For a math test," Eric said, settling back.

"And to think you have two daughters who'll be conspiring together in deeds probably much more devious than anything poor little Henry's ever thought of."

Groaning, Eric shut his eyes. "Maybe I can fake them out and pretend I have The Drop." He raised his arm and dropped it to the table.

"Remember, that one gets the big needle."

"Might be the preferable outcome. I mean, I'm not prepared, and I know they're probably making a list of all the ways they're going to pull things over on me when they're older."

"Why wait until they're older?" Dinah asked, heading to the door. "I have an idea they've already started."

"Not funny," he called after her. "Not funny at all."

She poked her head back in, smiling. "Wasn't meant to be."

Eric's response was to groan again. And pull a pillow over his head.

* * *

Her night at the hospital had been good. Working with Eric again even better. On impulse, while Dinah was halfway into chopping the romaine for that night's Caesar, she called him. "You busy tonight?" she asked, not sure why she was doing this. But doing it all the same.

"I, um…no, I don't suppose I am," he fumbled, sounding quite taken off guard. "Not unless there's an outbreak of The Drop."

"Want to come to dinner at the lodge?"

No response, and she was on the verge of embarrassment, and regret, for being so impulsive. Was this a mistake? Maybe she should have left well enough alone. But something was compelling her… "Bring the girls?" she added quickly, to save face. "I'd love to see them, love to have them take a tour of my kitchen." For a moment she considered adding his sister and niece to the guest list, but he agreed before she got that far with the invitation.

"Sure. We can come. I assume you're cooking?"

"Yes, but when I'm on a break…" What? What could she do with Eric and the twins on one of her fifteen-minute breaks? Or even on her thirty-minute meal break? Suddenly, what had seemed like a good idea didn't seem so good after all.

"You know they're going to want to wear their chef aprons," he said. "You've made quite an impression on them, and I don't think they've had those aprons off since they had their baking lesson."

"Well, maybe it's time to introduce them to the chef's hat." The conversation had turned into something about the girls, and Dinah had the impression Eric was awkward about this. No more than she was, probably. What a crazy thing to do, inviting him out this way, and when the conversation was over she was almost relieved. All awkwardness aside, though, they'd set a time, and she'd marked a reservation in the book for the best table in the house, which happened to be one of the closest to the kitchen. Then she continued chopping, taking care not let her mind wander too far lest she chop one of her fingers again.

"So, are you going to tell me what it's all about?" Angela asked her, thirty minutes later, when she was plopping down at the chef's table in the kitchen, trying, without much success, to make herself comfortable. "Because I recognize the mood. It's the pensive one."

"It's the pensive one because I did something dumb again."

"Does it have anything to do with Eric Ramsey?"

"I'm not interested in him the way you seem to think I am."

"And I didn't say you were. But you're mighty quick to bring it up, so I was just thinking that if you were interested in him the way *you think* I think you are…"

"Look, why don't you waddle your pregnant self back to your office and let me get the dinner service prep finished. OK?"

Angela laughed. "You were never good at hiding things, Dinah. That's why Mom always knew what we were up to. You gave us away every time, without saying a word, because it's right there, in your eyes. The whole story."

"Not the whole story," she argued.

"This time I think it's the whole story. You're interested, don't want to be, fighting not to be, and losing the fight. Am I right?"

"You know what I'm in the mood for?" Dinah purposely changed the flow of the conversation while clearing away the last of the romaine pieces and getting herself ready to cut up several loaves of crusty bread, soak them in garlic butter and bake them into croutons. She didn't want to talk about it, or think about it either. Didn't want it anywhere near her right now.

"I know what you're doing, changing the subject. But it won't work, Dinah. Not talking about it won't make it go away."

Dinah shot a scowl at her sister. "Not changing the subject. It got worn out and I was moving on to something nicer."

"What's nicer than talking about you falling for Eric Ramsey?"

Dinah reached out and patted her sister's belly. "This. I'm ready to become an aunt. So, how are you feeling? Any contractions? Any *anything*?"

"Actually, Gabby Evans came up to see me this morning. Bryce is still in the hospital in Salt Lake City, and he's doing remarkably well. She thinks he'll be home in another few days. But she came home to take care of a few things, and stopped by and had a look at me. She thinks I could go into labor any time. The baby's in position, and ready to come out and meet the world. In fact, if I haven't gone into labor in the next three or four days, she's going to induce me, or have someone else do it if she can't get here."

"Three or four days?" Suddenly, everything felt good. The world became better. "She'll get here, Angela. If there's any possible way, you know she'll get here."

"Well, if she doesn't, she doesn't. Bryce comes first for her, and I totally understand that."

Was she seeing a little apprehension coming over her sister? Considering what Angela had watched Gabby go through, Dinah wouldn't be surprised if her sister was scared to death and doing a very good job of hiding it. And considering that Angela was another victim of a cheating husband… "You're going to have a normal delivery," she said, sitting down next to her sister and pulling her into her arms. "Normal delivery, beautiful, healthy baby. We'll get through this together. Just the two of us. I promise."

"We'll get through it better if you tell me about your date tonight."

Dinah stiffened up, wondering if she still had time to call Eric's sister and niece and invite them, too. The more people there, the less the illusion of a *date*. "It's not a date. He's bringing his twins."

"Want to bet?" Angela struggled to a standing position, arched her back and headed back to her office, stopping before she was out of the kitchen. "It's OK to get involved, Dinah. I know I'm teasing you about it, and I'm probably the last person who should be giving anyone relationship advice seeing how my ex-husband is off on the slopes with a young ski bunny. But you know what? I want to be involved again. Brad hurt me, but he hasn't spoiled me because I know it's out there…true love, true happiness, all the things that make being involved with someone else good. It's there, and it *does* happen. And if it walked in the door right now, even in my condition, I'd give myself over to it in a heartbeat. So, don't reject it out of hand because you've had some bad experiences in the past. Maybe Eric isn't the one who'll be walking in your door someday. Maybe he is. But you'll never know if you don't leave that door open a crack."

Dinah wanted to take those words to heart. She truly did. But it seemed that her door swung one way. Out. She wasn't sure she wanted it to swing back in because, inevitably, any time it did, it swung right back out. And hurt her in such deep ways.

Maybe Eric would walk through her door, but she wasn't sure if she could survive him walking back out. It didn't matter, though, because she'd already convinced herself that a shut door was the best door. Even if Eric was standing on the other side of it, knocking.

CHAPTER FIVE

PREPARING a fresh salmon for the evening's sushi, Dinah was alternately slicing, discarding unusable pieces and reflecting on everything Angela had said. Her sister, so pregnant she could hardly move, with an ex-husband now flaunting his new relationship wherever he could, was still optimistic about love. That was the optimism Dinah wanted, the positive outlook that had eluded her for so long. Honestly, she envied her sister that. Wished she could be like her. Supposing Eric *did* want to get involved, not that she thought he would, but if, in some odd, twisted scheme of things that's what happened? What would be the worst outcome for her? A few weeks of something very nice with a man she found pleasant? She could do that for a few weeks. Go in with no expectations, come out unscathed.

See, that was her fundamental problem. She always had expectations. Even when she knew she shouldn't, she did. But what if she didn't? What if she could simply enter into something nice for a little while then walk away?

Yanking a piece of clear plastic from the roll, Dinah wrapped her fish in it then set about the task of removing scales from the second salmon. Thankless chore, smelly. Predictable outcome. People wouldn't care about the prep, they'd care about the end results. And that's where she always went wrong in her life—the end results. She cared too much, tried to make more happen than could, or would.

But could she enter into something without expecting anything at the end?

Grabbing up the de-boner, she looked at it for a moment then set it back with the rest of her knives. Even if she could get to the end without an expectation, there was always the possibility that Eric would want more. Then what?

"It's not going to happen," she muttered, totally disinterested in the whole salmon prep now. "Just not going to happen."

Her sous chef, a nice little man named Oswaldo— half a head shorter than she, long hair pulled back by a red bandana, pencil-thin mustache—gave her a quizzical look but didn't comment. Rather, he went about his sauce prep while she turned her attention to an asparagus risotto. Her concentration was lacking so badly, though, she couldn't even decide whether to use only the tender asparagus tips or peel and chop the whole stalk. In fact, all she could think of was Eric, his missing wedding ring…her lapse in sanity.

"You've already salted that," Oswaldo reminded her, trying to be discreet as he pushed the open salt container away from her.

"What?" she asked, trying to snap herself back into her work.

"Your risotto. Salted."

Dinah looked at the salt she'd pinched between her fingers and had been ready to dump into the risotto. This was her job now. Food prep. Slicing and dicing. *Salting*. And if she wasn't careful, she'd make a mess of that, too. "Look, I'm going to go take a short break. Can you cover for about fifteen minutes?"

Oswaldo nodded, and she didn't miss that little

glint in his eyes. He'd be happy to take over forever. Or, at least until Angela was back. And he was about to get his shot at it if she didn't shape up.

Tossing off her apron, Dinah thought about going back to her room, locking the door and climbing into bed. But fifteen minutes wasn't enough for that, so she opted for a quick walk to the rear of the lodge, and fifteen minutes in an employee-only area set up with outdoor chairs and tables. At the moment she was the only employee there, which suited her fine. Being alone, with nothing but a mountain slope and pine trees behind her, was a relief. No pressures there. Not to think. Not to react. Not to remember. Not to question herself.

"What am I doing?" she asked a chipmunk scurrying its way across the opening, heading straight for a pile of downed branches. "It's crazy. I know better. Maybe I should crawl under that pile of branches with you." Nice idea, except hiding never solved anything. Trouble was, she didn't know what did.

"So think of the moment," she said, switching her attention to a lone figure hiking his or her way up from a ravine in the distance. It was odd, seeing someone out here alone at this time of the day. Usually, they were in pairs, or more. In fact, she didn't recall seeing a single hiker out here anywhere, *ever*, so she watched the progress of the one in the distance, and got herself so caught up in his slow gait that she didn't even notice his pronounced limp until he was crossing over the back patch of lawn. Where, when he saw her, he collapsed in a heap.

Immediately, Dinah leapt up and ran to the man…a young man, not more than twenty, she guessed. Dropping to her knees beside him, she gave him a little shake on the shoulder. "Hey," she said, patting his cheeks, noticing the slight flutter of his eyelids. "Stay with me, do you hear?" Was it exhaustion? Dehydration? Immediately her fingers went to his pulse. "Stay awake."

He nodded in the affirmative, trying to speak, but a gash on his head, above his right eye, had been bleeding, substantially, and she wondered if he'd lost enough blood to make him woozy. Or was the head wound more serious than the super-ficial cut she could see?

"My brother…dad…" he whispered, his voice so low and raspy she was barely able to make out his words.

"We'll call them as soon as we get you taken care of." Her fingers pulled back his shirt so she could have a look at the way he moved air in and out of his lungs. His pulse was too fast, his breathing too shallow. He could have been too pale underneath the layers of dirt and blood but she couldn't tell. So she did a quick assessment, felt his arms, his legs, probed his abdomen to see if it was distended or rigid. It was not. "Where do you hurt?" she finally asked him.

"Please, my dad and my brother, they…" His eyes fluttered shut, and he fought to open them again, but it was a losing battle as he lapsed into unconsciousness.

Immediately, Dinah clicked on her cell phone and speed-dialed the first name at the top. By the time the first ring sounded, she was already going through the young man's pockets, looking for identification. First his jacket pockets, then his cargo pants…pants with numerous pockets, visible and hidden, everywhere.

"You having second thoughts about our date tonight?" Eric asked rather than saying hello.

"I have an unconscious young man, age approximately twenty, on the back lawn of the lodge. He walked here then collapsed when I got to him. Head wound, can't tell how serious, but he's done some extensive bleeding. Tachycardia, shallow respirations. Eyes responding, but very sluggish." She found his wallet in a zipper pocket midway down to his knee and pulled it out. "His belly's not rigid, there are no obvious breaks, at least nothing compound, and he stayed conscious only a few seconds before he went out on me so I don't have any idea what happened to him." One glance at his driver's license, and she added, "He's not a local. According to his identification, he's from Canada…Ontario."

"I'm on my way," Eric said. "Get him as stable as possible, and I'll make the rest of the arrangements from here."

"It's bad, Eric. I think it's really bad." She clicked off with Eric and called the main desk at the lodge. "Hello, Redmond," she said to the concierge who answered. "This is Dinah, from the kitchen. I have a critically injured young man out on the back lawn—"

"I'll call for help," he interrupted.

"No, listen to me. I've already called. What I need from you are blankets and a couple of pillows. Immediately." The boy was already shocky, but warming him up and elevating his legs could lessen the trauma, help keep him stable until Eric got there. "And I need someone to go and find his family. His last name is Dawson. This is Troy, and he asked for his brother and father."

When she clicked off, she didn't have to wait for more than a minute before one of the lodge workers came running with an armload of blankets, followed by another one carrying pillows. Redmond followed up with a first-aid kit and several bottles of water, and he was flanked by two more workers who had come only in case more help was needed.

"We've got someone going up to his cabin now. According to the registration, they're staying in one of the family cabins. And they're a family of five—husband, wife, three children."

Dinah had a sinking feeling that maybe Troy's

brother and father had been with him, that they might have been injured, too. But she didn't want to voice that opinion and cause a panic. Best to leave the search to Eric, should a search become necessary.

"Dr. Ramsey called us. His ETA is two minutes," Redmond informed her.

"How?" she said, then looked up as Redmond pointed to the helicopter coming into view.

By the time it had landed on the east lawn, which had been cleared of guests by another one of the lodge workers, Dinah had Troy's feet propped up, and had him well tucked into his blankets. His pulse was still too fast, too thready, and he wasn't responding at all to her attempts to rouse him by calling his name or by pinching him. It was a serious head injury, possible fracture, with bleeding and swelling. She was convinced of it.

"Any change?" Eric shouted. He was running hard in her direction, carrying a medical bag.

"No response."

He dropped to his knees, and handed his medical bag over to her. Immediately she went for the blood-pressure cuff. Thirty seconds later, she looked over at him. "It's ninety over sixty." Too low.

"Pupils are responsive, but very slow," Eric said.

Bad sign. But not the worst-case scenario by a long shot.

"So was he coherent when you found him?"

"He was walking…more like staggering up the trail." She pointed to the south end of the lawn. "I watched him for a while because he seemed to be moving so slowly. But I didn't know he was injured. Then as he made the clearing, even though I couldn't tell, I had the feeling that something wasn't right. So I ran down there, and he…he collapsed. Wanted me to tell his brother and dad. At least that's what I thought he wanted. But, Eric, I might be wrong. I have this hunch that his dad and brother are out there somewhere, and he was the one who was coming for help."

"Damn," Eric muttered. He looked up at Redmond. "Does anyone here know for sure? Has anyone seen his family?"

"We're tracking them down now. Nobody's at the cabin, but one of our guests saw the mother and daughter go off together earlier. Didn't see the father and sons, though. So I've got my people knocking on doors right now."

"Then they could be out there?" Dinah asked, looking out to the vast expanse of woods around her, and the never-ending mountains beyond that.

"I'm going to send him down to the hospital right now, go down there with him, then I'm coming back, getting Neil up here with me, and we're going to start a search and rescue, unless I hear something different in the meantime." He motioned over two of the hotel workers, instructed them to retrieve the stretcher from the helicopter then he made a phone call to the hospital. Two minutes later Troy Dawson, who'd yet to regain consciousness, was on his way to the helicopter, while Eric lagged behind for a moment. "I think I may have to take a rain check on that dinner later on," he said, grabbing his medical bag and spinning away.

"I want to do this," Dinah said, practically running to keep up with him. She was tall, but her strides didn't come close to matching Eric's, especially when he was in a hurry.

"What?" he shouted, the noise of the helicopter getting louder the closer they got.

"Help with the rescue," she shouted back. "I want to be part of it." Because she felt obligated. Because Troy had been trying to tell her something and she hadn't been able to keep him conscious long enough to find out what. Hadn't been able to hold on to Molly long enough...

"Can you find the trail he came up on?" he yelled, then motioned her away as he climbed into the helicopter. "That could get us off to a faster start if we know where to start looking."

She was still nodding when the helicopter lifted off, watching it disappear over the older Sister in a matter of seconds. She had to find the trail... First thing she did was run to the kitchen to tell Oswaldo he would be in charge of the cooking. Next, she phoned Angela to let her know what was going on, and make sure she wasn't in labor. Then she changed into hiking boots, put on a comfortable pair of jeans and layered on a couple of shirts with a green sweater, tied her hair up in a bandana and scrounged for anything that might be of help in a mountain rescue, even though she'd never been on one before. She had her medical bag... bandages, scissors, stethoscope. More bulk than she wanted to carry, but...

Out the door in a blink, she ran to the gift shop and grabbed up a souvenir backpack.

"You can't take that!" the teenage clerk exclaimed while Dinah was dumping her med supplies inside, totally ignoring the girl's protests. After her own supplies, she added a lightweight blanket she found on one of the gift-shop shelves, as well as a flashlight, a small travel pillow, and several plastic bottles of water. On impulse, she scooped up a handful of candy bars and several pairs of fluorescent pink shoe-laces popular with children. She had no idea what she'd need them for, but she felt better with a full pack.

"I said, you can't take that!" The clerk was now yelling. "I'm calling Security." Which she did. But the kindly old security officer, a man called Wallace Gilpin, who'd been perched on a chair almost outside the door, reading a magazine, scooped some packages of premade crackers with peanut butter from the gift shop shelf and handed them to Dinah.

"Protein," he said. "Not much, but it could help." Next, he dug a gold cigarette lighter from his pocket and handed it to her. "You might be needing this, too. But, please, take care of it. It belonged to my father." With the lighter, he handed her his magazine. "And this, just in case you need a fire starter."

"The brother and father were with him," Redmond called from across the lobby. "And no one has seen them come back. We've sent someone down to the village to find Troy's mother and sister. I've got a cell phone number for them, but I thought having someone tell them in person was better than a phone call."

"Well, I'm going on ahead to find the trail." In the whole scheme of a search-and-rescue operation, it would probably be a small contribution, but saving time had to be good. Especially with only a few hours of light left.

"Use this," Redmond said, handing her a walkie-talkie. "Dr. Ramsey has his own communication, but it doesn't hurt to have a back-up. And you won't get cell reception once you're too far away from the lodge. But these carry for quite a way."

"Are you sure you know what you're doing?" Angela asked. She'd wandered down to the lobby, where Wallace was already scooting a chair in her direction.

"No, I'm not sure. But the one thing I do know is that I can't sit around and do nothing. Eric needs me to find the trail, and if there's a chance that Troy has a brother or father out there, and they need help…" She ran to her sister, gave her a quick kiss on the cheek. "Let Redmond know if you need me…one twinge, Angela, and I'll be back. Promise?"

Angela lifted her hand to wave, but Dinah was gone before she saw it. Running across the lawn, she discovered at least a dozen different trails, all starting at approximately the same place, all leading to vastly different areas. Suddenly she wasn't so sure where she'd seen Troy. At least four of the trail heads seemed likely, which meant she was going to have to go further. See if she could find traces of anything…blood, something he might have dropped.

Half way across the lawn, her cell phone jingled. "We've got Troy in the emergency room, and I'll be back in a few minutes. Any luck finding the right trail?"

"When I find the trail, will you let me go out with you?" she asked.

"We'll talk about it."

"I want to go, Eric. I feel…responsible. If I could have kept Troy talking, I might have discovered where his brother and father are. Or, if I'd noticed him sooner, gotten to him quicker…" So many things bothered her, but the thing that bothered her most of all was thinking about someone else being lost out there. "I want to go, and I don't want to talk about it."

"On my rescues, you follow my orders, Dinah."

"I'm a nurse, Eric. I always follow orders."

"But you're not experienced in mountain rescue."

"Then send me back if I get in the way or impede the rescue. But give me a chance. I need to…need to do this. The idea that a young boy is out there somewhere…" She shut her eyes, trying to not picture all the possibilities of trouble that boy, and his father, could be in. But in the dark of her eyelids, she saw bad things. "I have to do this, Eric." But she wouldn't, if he didn't want her. Because she was a good nurse. Because she knew how to take orders.

"Find the trail, Dinah. Just find the right trail."

The first two trail heads turned up nothing. She went some way on each, looking for clues that Troy might have come that way, and found nothing. It was on the third trail she discovered fresh drops of blood…probably from the gash on Troy's head. "Hello," she shouted, on the off chance that the Dawson family was within hearing distance. Of course, no one answered, not that she'd really expected them to. But on impulse, before she headed down that trail, she tied a pink shoelace to a tree branch so Eric would know where she was starting. Then she plunged into the woods, looking for more signs that Troy had come this way.

There were signs everywhere. Scuff marks in the dirt indicated he'd been dragging himself exactly where she was tracking. And she found more blood droplets, and other larger marks in the dirt…handprints? Perhaps where he'd stumbled and fallen?

But there were only signs of one person coming through here. She'd hoped for more, hoped that a few feet into the woods she'd find Troy's brother, or dad. Maybe with a broken leg. Something incapacitating, but not too serious. Of course, that didn't turn out to be the case, but she refused to allow early discouragement to get her down. Rather, she followed the obvious trail, one that was easy to read. Bargaining with God for an early success.

Everything reminded her of a giant jigsaw puzzle, and she was the only one there to solve it. "Solve it," she whispered, bending down to have a closer look at the broken frond of a fern. Nothing. It wasn't broken. Just not fully developed. And nothing else around her gave her a clue, which meant, to the untrained eye, the trail had run out not far after it had started. Maybe she'd gone the wrong way? Or taken a wrong turn?

Maybe she was letting the Dawson family down the way she'd let Molly down.

Suddenly a cold chill swept over her. What was she doing, thinking she could be of use out here, as a nurse, as…anything? In the distance, through the trees, she could still see the lodge, and the search activity mounting in the parking lot. It was time to go back. Raw, bitter discouragement *was* beginning to overtake her because she wanted to make a difference and she wasn't.

"It's not easy," Eric said, suddenly stepping up behind her. "It's never about strolling through the woods until you come across your victim."

"But I thought that if I found the trail…"

"You did find the trail," he said, holding up the pink shoelace marker. "This is it."

In her mind's eye, the scenario played out happily. She and Eric would turn the next bend in the trail and find Troy's dad and brother sitting there, waiting for someone to find them. They'd be alive, slightly damaged, but good. Except the story she saw etched on Eric's face told her something altogether different. "Worst-case scenario?" she asked.

"We run out of daylight without finding them. Or we find them and they're…"

This was going to be a long, hard search and the hard lump in her stomach was telling her the outcome might not be the one she wanted. "I'm right behind you," she whispered, as Eric took the lead. Instinctively, she looked up to see the sky, but the canopy of leaves overhead totally blotted out all but a few splotchy patches of light. "And I can run, Eric. I won't slow you down."

She followed him for the next twenty minutes, alternately running and stopping to assess the trail. Words between them were spared in order to conserve breath, but she did what Eric did. She observed everything, looking off to the sides of the trail, looking up, looking down. Once, when they stopped to take a drink of water, she asked the question she feared asking. "What happens if we have to go back?"

"We could lose the trail. It could be wiped out by a light rain, or a good wind. Since it's spring, that's highly likely."

"And you don't stay out after dark?"

"It depends on the situation. Normally we don't keep the volunteers out. Too many people out in the dark becomes a risk factor itself. But I have some specialists who go out at night, and Neil's getting them ready to go right now. He'll send them on an alternate trail, one that parallels us."

"All I can think about is that if we have to turn back, what if Troy's brother and father are only over the next hill? How do you make the decision to quit, and start again tomorrow, when you could be so close?"

"Judgment…experience. I don't ever like to quit, but if I'm leading the field team, I have to think about their safety first. Neil and I have a good group of volunteers who'll put their own lives at risk to save someone else, and it's up to me to make sure they don't put their lives at risk." He took one more swig of water from the plastic bottle, held it out to her, and when she refused another drink he capped it and clipped it to his belt. "It's only going to get rougher up ahead, Dinah. We need to cover more area, faster, because daylight is getting to be a huge factor now."

"Am I slowing you down so far?" she asked.

"No, but I don't want to make this miserable for you, since you've never done this type of thing before."

"What makes me miserable is knowing that…" She swallowed hard, trying to fight back the emotion. Eric didn't need her to be emotional out here, didn't need her thinking with her heart when a search and rescue such as this followed logical, ordered procedures. "I can do this, Eric." She trusted that completely.

Actually, she trusted Eric with all her heart. Too bad her heart hadn't found him when she could have given it to him. Because now, there was nothing left to give away except tatters. But, then, Eric had a few tatters of his own. So maybe knowing she couldn't have him was part of the attraction she felt for him. If nothing else, it was safe.

Safe. Yes, she wanted to be safe. But how safe? "And I'm ready to run."

He reached out and squeezed her hand. "When this is over, remind me to tell you how amazing you are."

"I've got part of the team going up to the ridge, looking for a vantage point," Neil relayed to Eric. "We might get lucky and find them by looking down, if we have enough daylight left. Oh, and Redmond's just heard from the boy's mother. She said her husband and the boys were going out to camp, but she didn't know where, except they'd mentioned renting a rubber raft. Troy is eighteen, by the way, and his brother, Shawn, is twelve. William, the father, is forty, and in good health."

"Where is she right now?" Eric asked.

"She's gone to the hospital to be with Troy. He hasn't come round yet, and it's not looking good. Scan shows a skull fracture, and they're getting ready to fly him down to Salt Lake City for surgery. He's got a subdural hematoma, too. Mrs Dawson will be going with him."

"Damn," Eric muttered. It would have been so easy to let the concierge know where they were going. But people came out here and did… foolish things. Foolish, like taking two sons and going off God only knew where for an adventure. Skilled outdoorsmen left word, drew their course on maps and left them behind as a reference. They checked in with the national park authorities. Told their wives. But amateurs went and assumed things would work out. Sometimes they prepared properly as far as the gear they took, sometimes they didn't. More often than not, they didn't do the proper research, didn't tell anybody anything. More often than not, they were the ones he was sent to rescue. When there were fatalities, they were the ones who usually died.

No, he didn't have a good feeling about this at all. Then he thought about Dinah again, and had to smile. For an amateur in outdoor rescue, she'd done it all right, sort of. Her inexperience taken into account, she'd left her markers for him, kept in touch, gathered up odd, but good supplies, according to the security guard. Good instincts. Untrained, but with a natural knack. Someone to train properly in rescue later on. If she stayed…

"Is Dinah keeping up with you? Because I

could get someone from the hospital to run the base camp and come in to pair up with you. Or…" Neil chuckled. "Maybe you'd rather be pairing up with her?"

Eric studied her for a moment, standing off by herself, looking in every direction, studying, taking it all in. "What I'd rather be doing is having a nice quiet dinner—"

"With Dinah?" Neil interrupted.

"With Dinah," Eric admitted. "But right now we're taking a water break, eating protein bars, and getting ready to run another mile or two."

"Toward the river," Neil said. "If they were carrying a rubber raft…"

"Then they wouldn't have gone too far."

"Maybe the rapids?"

Eric cringed at the thought. Inexperience on the rapids equaled tragedy. "Let's hope they were smarter than that."

"Well, I've got twenty people out, and another group ready to go. Let me know what you need." With that, Neil clicked off and suddenly it was just the two of them, alone. No civilization around to buffer them.

"Ready to go again?" Eric called. Damn, he

admired her. He was working her hard, pushing her far more than he should push anyone without the kind of experience he needed from a volunteer out here, yet he knew she wouldn't let him down. There was nothing in Dinah he didn't trust and he only wished she trusted herself half as much as he did.

"Ready," she called, slinging her pack back over her shoulder. "How are we doing on daylight?"

He glanced up at the sky. It would be dark too soon...a sobering thought. He hated the night because that's when victims died most often. Maybe because with sunlight there was hope. Maybe because with the night came the feeling of cold, lonely desperation. "Not good. But the river's not too far off and we should make that in good time, and hope they didn't go much farther than the first entry point we'll come to." He glanced down at the ground, at a speck of blood splattered against a brown leaf. "Damn," he muttered. They were running out of time. Everything inside him was screaming that, loud and clear.

"Well, I'm up for a nice, hard run. Ready whenever you are."

Dinah Corday was intense, dedicated...like no

other woman he'd ever encountered, and he wasn't sure how to handle her…or handle himself around her. But the one sure thing amidst all his confused feelings was that he felt more alive around her than he'd felt in years. After Patricia, he'd spent so much time feeling lost, feeling alone. Feeling like he'd lost his only chance at true happiness when she'd died.

But Dinah stirred things in him. Familiar things as well as things he'd never felt before. Things that made him want to crawl up in a ball and pray they would go away, and things he wanted to shout about from the top of the older Sister. He was happy. He felt disloyal. Mostly, though, he liked being with Dinah, however it happened.

He fingered the shoelace in his pocket as he headed off down the trail they'd been following for the past hour. Couldn't help but smile as he twisted the shoelace around his index finger.

CHAPTER SIX

ERIC clicked on his radio. "Look, Neil, I think he was coming from the river and got turned around. It's easy to do up here, since this is close to where the river cuts in. What I'm not seeing though is any sign that three people came through here together recently. So I think Troy taking this trail was an accident. I don't think we're going to find anything on it, which means I'm going off trail and heading straight over to the river."

Neil's expletive was brittle and explosive. "Look, I've got the team on the ridge now, but they're too far away, not going to get to the river before you do, and I don't think you're going to get to a point where you can meet up with them before I have to call them back in for the night."

"Well, I'm betting that the Dawsons wouldn't have gone too far upriver. Maybe as far as the rapids. It's still a good hike up there, but I think can make it before dark, and I'm not inclined to turn around."

"The rapids are another hour ahead of you, and I'm not happy having you and Dinah out there after dark, as Dinah isn't experienced."

Dinah listened to the exchange, following along behind Eric who was still going forward at a fast pace. He had an uncanny sense about this, like he anticipated what he was about to find before he found it. And he didn't talk. Not a word, except when he reported back to Neil every few minutes. Every ounce of his physical energy, as well as his mental concentration, was spent on the search, and he was so pulled into it, Dinah didn't dare speak lest she snapped his focus the way the twigs snapped under their boots. In fact, she was almost afraid to breathe in case that little distraction knocked him out of the moment.

It was an amazing thing to watch. This wasn't Eric the doctor. It was Eric the hunter. The rescuer. A man who took away her breath each and every time he paused to look at something— a disturbed leaf, an imprint in the dirt. A man who took away her breath for no other reason than he was Eric Ramsey.

"We're going to climb," he continued to Neil. "That'll cut off more than half the time, and I think we'll still have enough light left to get us all the way down to the river. Why don't you go ahead and send the second team out, have them come in from the north? Then we'll be good for a while."

"The second team?" Dinah asked, after he'd finished talking to Neil.

"My night crew. It still gets cold up here after dark, too cold if either of the Dawsons are seriously injured, so we're going to stay out for a while. Are you up to it?"

"I'm not quitting, Eric. If you go on, so do I. But what if they're not at the rapids?" One guess out of so many places scared her because right now, in the near-darkness, the woods around them seemed so much bigger than they did during the day, and trying to place Troy in one particular spot was such a daunting task. But Eric was experienced. His guesses… hunches… were based on such a solid foundation she had to trust him.

Trust. There was that frightening word again.

It seemed to come up so much when she was with Eric.

"Sometimes you just have to guess. Three people and a rubber raft...inexperienced. The raft is heavy. If you want to put it in the water you're not going to spend the whole day hiking, trying to find a good starting place, but you want to go far enough to feel that you're really out in the wilderness. If they got as far as the rapids they wouldn't have gone beyond that because even the most inexperienced outdoorsmen wouldn't shoot those rapids in a rubber raft. So that would put them someplace downriver from there. Until now, the river was too far off trail, but it starts to cut back in just east of here, so I think they would have tried rafting somewhere between here and the rapids, hopefully closer to this point than the rapids."

"Well, I'm prepared to stay out here all night, if that's what we have to do. You know, I've packed food, water. A blanket and a pillow, too."

"A pillow? You brought a pillow?"

"I thought I might need it. And it could come in handy, couldn't it? I mean, my pink shoelaces did."

* * *

"Don't look down," he said to Dinah. "You'll get dizzy, so look up at me, do what I tell you, and you'll be fine."

Look down? It was hard looking anywhere with her eyes squeezed tightly shut. "Isn't there another way to get to the bottom from up here?" As rockfaces went, this one was small. She knew that. But she'd never climbed anything more than a flight of stairs, and this was just plain scary. That, plus the fact she wasn't especially fond of heights. She would have preferred letting Eric do the climbing while she took the long way down, walking. But he wouldn't hear of it. Wouldn't leave her alone. And time was running out. That was the winning argument. Shawn Dawson and his father needed help, and if they didn't take this shortcut to the river, their rescue efforts would have to end for the day. Thinking about the young boy out there, hurt, scared… that's what propelled her to the edge of the cliff, and had her standing there, toes over the edge, trying not to look down.

"So how do you just step off the edge?" she asked, forcing herself another inch forward.

"You trust me. I've got you tied, you'll be fine. And this is a very easy beginner rock to climb."

"If you want to climb," she muttered, bracing herself for the inevitable.

"Turn around, watch me, and I'll lower you over."

"And if you drop me?"

"I've never dropped anybody before."

If only he knew how much of an issue trust was for her. Of course, this was not a question of emotional trust. The worst she'd get from this would be some cuts and bruises. They healed. Emotional bruises didn't, so this was a far easier trust to have. "OK, well…" She turned around, grabbed hold of her ropes and backed to the edge.

"You're going to be fine, so just lower yourself over the edge and walk, don't bounce, down the side. Trust me, Dinah, this is easy. You can do it."

"Easy for you to say," Dinah grumbled, then drew in a deep breath and took a big leap of faith over the edge. Literally.

The first step off was the worst. The immediate sensation was that she was falling…nothing between her and the ground but air, lots and lots of air.

"You're doing fine," he called. "Just don't swing too much, and you'll be down before you know it."

"Trust him," she muttered out loud, as her feet connected with the rockface and she was grounded again. "Trust him…trust him…" In a way, it was like falling in love—that first feeling of falling or floating, the eventual sure footing. Of course, in her case, she always plummeted hard after the first few steps. Never did find her sure footing. "Trust him…" Those two words were becoming her mantra.

"Keep going," he said, looking down over the edge at her. "You're doing a fantastic job."

"Like you'd say anything else to someone who was dangling in midair." When she finally gathered enough courage to take a look at that *fantastic* job he claimed she was doing, she saw she'd gone only a few feet. Problem was, it was a short forty-foot drop, total. Something that should take her only a couple of minutes, according to Eric. But those forty feet were insurmountable, and she was stuck swinging in midair, couldn't get back up, couldn't force herself to continue on down.

Suddenly, panic turned her lungs into lead. Nothing was moving in and out. Her head was getting light, her fingers and toes tingly. It had to be a panic attack coming on. She'd never had one, but she recognized the symptoms. Dangling off the side of a cliff in mid-panic. She *had* to trust him, there was no other way to get out of this, to get on with the rescue. The rescue…that's where she had to focus her thoughts. Shawn needed her. His father needed her.

Eric trusted her to do this…trusted her.

About a minute into the ordeal, when her lungs finally gave out and forced her to breathe again, she realized she'd been biting down on her lips so hard they were bleeding. But something else was happening. Suspended there, as she was, a feeling of exhilaration was coming over her. Her slow progress was mounting into an unexpected victory, not only of will but of trust, and by the time she'd reached firm ground at the bottom, she was ready to have another go at it. But looking up, watching Eric scale down with the skill and grace of an aerial artist, she wondered if she'd ever have the chance to do that again. With Eric. Because it was his trust in her as much as her trust in him that had got her to the bottom.

"You OK?" he asked, as he hit the ground.

Immediately, he grabbed hold of her arm and pulled her into him.

She went willingly, fell against his chest and caught her breath there. Lingered a moment longer as the adrenaline rush passed. "That wasn't so bad," she said, still a little winded.

"Then we'll do it again sometime, when I've had more time to teach you."

"I'd like that, and next time I won't be such a baby." She hoped.

"Trial by fire isn't the easiest way to learn. But you did a good job, Dinah."

Trial by fire…that's all her life had been since she'd been in White Elk. And she'd plunged into some very dangerous fires lately. "Trial by fire might not be the easiest way to learn, but it sure does make you move forward, like it or not."

After their quick embrace he went right back to work, gathering in his ropes. Once he'd wound them over his shoulder, he pointed in the direction of the river. She could hear rushing waters from where she was. In a way, it reminded her of the unexpected power she found in Eric. On the surface he was tranquil, but when she got close she sensed the currents rippling in him, the ones she didn't expect, like the currents that surprised her now, in the sounds of the river.

She hoped they would find Troy's brother and father once they reached the river's edge, but the chances of that happening weren't too good. And the real test was going to be figuring out which way to go—upriver, or down. The real test of this rescue, the real test of her life. Which way to go?

They hiked for several minutes, Eric in the lead, Dinah following, flanking him off to the left by about twenty yards. Not close, but not so far from him that she couldn't see him. She kept her eyes darting back and forth, looking for signs of life, signs that someone had been there recently. Imitating Eric in her actions. But since this was not a blazed trail, she didn't expect to find much. And once again she didn't speak, barely dared breathe for fear that, even at this distance away from him, if she broke Eric's concentration, he might miss something.

Then suddenly, something caught her attention. It was still another few feet off to her left, but she darted off course and dropped to her knees when she came upon it. A shoe. A single shoe, size eight, boys'. Fairly new. "Eric!" she called. "Over here!"

Eric barely looked at the shoe. Rather, he rushed on by her. "Shawn!" he called, then listened for a moment. "William! Can you hear me?"

To her ears there was no response, but something propelled Eric to a spot another hundred feet away. "Shawn, can you hear me?" he called. "Shawn!"

Again, she heard nothing…but she listened, dear God she listened hard. "Shawn!" she yelled, standing back up and turning in circles. "Shawn, William! We're here to help you! Can you hear us?"

She knew children, knew how they responded. When they were frightened, they hid. Shawn would be scared to death. But the question was, if his father couldn't respond, would Shawn be able to respond to them if he could hear them? If that was his shoe…

"Dinah, over here!" Eric yelled, motioning her over to an outcropping of rocks. They were practically at the river's edge now. And that's where they found the second shoe. It was on the foot of a young boy. Eric was already making the initial assessment—taking a pulse. Dinah flew into action, pulling her flashlight from her backpack and looking for pupillary reaction. Normal. His respirations were weak, though. And his skin was chilled to the touch. Even though Troy had obviously wrapped his own jacket over his brother before he'd gone for help, Shawn was suffering mild hypothermia.

"Shawn," Eric said, patting his cheeks, trying to awaken him.

"Shock?" she asked.

"And mild exposure." He picked up the totally full bottle of water Troy had obviously left with his brother. It was still full. "Dehydration's setting in."

"Broken leg." Dinah ran her hands lightly over the boy's extremities, frowned then grimaced. "Both legs, I think."

"No distension in his abdomen," Eric responded. "But he could still have internal injuries." He looked up at the rocks, expelling a frustrated sigh. "Wish we knew what happened to him."

"Shawn, can you hear us? Can you wake up and tell us what happened to you?"

In response his eyelids fluttered, but his eyes didn't fully open.

"I think Troy must have carried him this far, then left him where he thought it was safe. Probably because he couldn't carry him any further." Eric grabbed the walkie-talkie and clicked it on. "We have one victim, twelve-year-old male, unconscious, possible broken legs, possible internal injuries. I'm going to splint his legs and leave Dinah here while I go and look for his father, unless the other crew gets in here before then. What's their estimated time?"

"Not going to make it before dark," Neil said.

"Well, have them keep to the river. And get a helicopter in here, because I'd rather evacuate the boy as soon as possible, while we still have a little light, and deal with the father when we find him." Eric and Neil discussed arrangements while Dinah snipped the fabric back from Shawn's legs to get a better look. What she saw made her cringe. Both were definitely broken, so badly that the angles of the breaks were obvious even though the skin itself wasn't broken. This poor child would require numerous surgeries and months and months of physical therapy.

But he was alive, and while she wrapped Eric's thermal rescue blanket around him and placed her little travel pillow under his head, the familiar pang hit her. This was what she needed to do— take care of children. "Shawn, you're safe now. Just stay with us, and we're going to take you to a hospital not too far from here. Your mother is already there, with Troy. She's waiting for you."

For the next few minutes, sitting and talking to Shawn the way she was, taking his vitals and cleaning various scrapes and cuts on his arms and face, she thought about where her heart truly was. No matter what she'd told Eric, no matter how much she wanted to believe she had no heart for this, she did. There was no denying it. "Can a helicopter land here?" She asked Eric, after he'd clicked off from Neil.

"There's a place, downriver, about half a mile. We'll have to get him ready to travel then get him down to the pick-up point. Neil's going to fly in and take him from there."

"Have they called his mother?" she asked Eric.

"I'm sure someone will."

"But she needs to know. Right now. Someone who loves this child needs to know he's alive!"

Eric studied her for a moment then smiled. "Right away," he said gently. "We'll let her know right away." He clicked his radio back on to Neil. "You think of the things no one else does," he said to Dinah. Then he gave her a curious look, but said nothing.

"What?" she finally asked him.

"You'd make a wonderful mother."

She looked down at Shawn, and automatically took hold of his wrist, feeling for a pulse. "I need to be stable in my own life before I can be responsible for another person. And in case you haven't noticed, my life isn't too stable these days."

"You underestimate yourself, Dinah."

"Or maybe you overestimate me."

"Actually, I think I estimate you just right. And what I've estimated so far is about perfect."

"Don't," she whispered to him raggedly. "Please, don't have expectations of me."

It took approximately thirty minutes to get Shawn stabilized and down to the rescue spot on a makeshift stretcher Eric lashed together from tree limbs. It was an amazing thing, watching him. He was so resourceful in the woods, not a moment of hesitation. Born to do this, she thought as she fashioned splints to the boy's legs.

"He's warming up," she called, as Eric was cutting the last of the tree limbs. "Pulse is evening out, blood pressure's up."

"I just heard from Neil and they'll be en route as soon as we signal. Also, the second crew found William Dawson and they're taking him out right now. He's about a mile upriver, conscious, extreme hypothermia, back injury, possible internal injuries. The raft got caught in river debris, they got tossed around pretty badly on the rocks. He was trapped in the water, leg caught between a couple of rocks, couldn't get loose, so Troy tried to carry Shawn out…"

Not a great ending, but not a horrible one, either. For that, she was relieved. "Your father and brother are fine," she told Shawn, as Eric came back with the last of the tree limbs.

"We're going to take you to the hospital, and you'll be fine in no time. Just a little while longer…" She glanced up at Eric, his rugged form stunning, even though the only light on him now came from their flashlights. "We did it. I mean, we actually did it."

"You've got good instincts out here."

"I was so afraid I'd slow you down, or do

something wrong, something that could have been dangerous."

He bent, took Shawn's pulse then steadied the boy's neck as they lifted him onto the makeshift stretcher. "This is what you need to do, Dinah. Rescue, nursing…either one, or both. You're wasting your time in that kitchen."

"And my ex-fiancé, Charles, said I was wasting my time as a nurse."

"Then he's an idiot on two counts. One, for letting you go. Two, for not recognizing how extraordinarily talented you are."

Together, they carried Shawn to the rendezvous point, where Neil met them and took over from there. The night had finally dropped down on them, and Dinah felt a huge sense of relief once she saw the stretcher being lifted into the helicopter, with Shawn strapped in. She didn't glance away until the chopper had made a wide turn and was headed away from the river, its lights a shining beacon of success against the black sky. That's when the true feeling of relief washed over her that all three of the Dawsons would be safe. That's also when her knees gave out and she sat down, cross-legged, on a boulder near the river.

Eric propped himself against the rock, but didn't sit. Rather, he leaned, arms folded casually across his chest. "From here, winding our way back along the river, it's going to take about three hours."

Dinah's reply was a groan.

"We could cut back through the woods and save some time, but I'm not especially interested in a tough hike at this point, which is what that would be. So…"

"So, let me rest for a few minutes," she said, every ounce of tiredness creaking its way into her voice.

"Do you like camping?" he asked.

"You mean, staying here tonight?"

"Get a good night's sleep, head back in the morning."

"I'm not much of a camper," she said. "But I wasn't much of a climber either, and that turned out pretty well, considering how I was scared to death."

"Well, there's nothing to be afraid of out here. We'll build a campfire…"

If it weren't for the fact that she was weary to the bone, that could have sounded romantic.

"I could camp."

"You could do anything you set your mind to.

I'm not sure you believe that, but I believe in you out here, Dinah. Depended on you as much as I depend on any one of my rescue team."

"You shouldn't have," she whispered. "In the end, it just doesn't work out. I know we had a good outcome today, but maybe it could have been better if you'd put your trust in someone else."

Eric expelled an impatient breath. "See, that's how you always react. You pull back. Don't want anybody to trust you. It's damn frustrating, Dinah, because I see how good you are. Everybody sees that but you, and I don't know what it would take to make you see the same thing we all see in you."

"What you see in me isn't real," she said, her voice totally flat.

"Why, Dinah? Tell me what this is about? Let me understand."

"There's nothing to understand."

"That's you pulling back, Dinah. Or pushing me away. And I want to know why. We've worked together, saved lives together… I need to know why the things you do so well are the things that make you so sad."

"Because I lost a little girl once, Eric. A patient. Her name was Molly, and nobody loved her enough to stay with her. She was abandoned, and forgotten because she wasn't lucky enough to have been bestowed with anything that could be construed as a good quality of life."

"What was wrong with her?" he asked, his voice going from agitated to gentle.

"Anencephalic. On life support for her few short weeks."

"I'm sorry," he whispered.

"So was I. And in the end it broke my heart. She trusted me. I mean, I know that most people would say she didn't even know I was there, but I think she knew, and I couldn't…" She drew in a deep, ragged breath. "After it was over, I just sat there for hours, holding on. I wouldn't let her go…couldn't. They tried to take her away from me and I couldn't…wouldn't let go. I mean, I knew she'd died. Knew all along she couldn't survive. But in the end, I just…" Tears broke free from her eyes, and she swiped at them with the cuff of her sleeve. "They had to physically remove me from the room. They took her away from me and sedated me. Afterwards, Charles recommended I take a long leave of absence, or reconsider whether or not I should even be a nurse because he thought I might not be emotionally fit to care for patients, getting involved the way I did. And he might be right. I…I don't know. But Molly's the reason I couldn't walk away from this rescue. It's not in me to leave a child who needs my help. And she's also the reason I can't get involved…because I'm afraid my emotions might cloud my judgment. In a kitchen, the worst I can do is burn my sauce. But in a hospital…"

"I'm so sorry for your loss," he said, his voice so controlled it was barely audible against the night sounds beginning to start up from the bushes and trees.

"I expect you've had your share of patient losses. And I know it's not easy. But for me, I've never gotten past the place where it's personal. Taking care of every one of my patients…my children…is so personal. I can't detach myself the way some of my colleagues did."

"Which is what makes you better than just about any nurse I've ever seen. Which is why your little Molly knew you, Dinah. She felt your heart, felt your love. Charles was wrong. Getting involved is what makes you so good."

"But getting involved broke my heart."

"Because you had no one there to support you. And I'm sorry you didn't. You deserved better, Dinah." He lowered himself to the ground and pulled her down with him. Then sitting there, at the base of the rock at the river's edge, he pulled her into his arms. "You really deserved better."

"Why do you believe in me so much?" she whispered.

"Because until you came along, I was still a married man. In my heart, I'd never seen the need to be any other way. It worked. I got along. Then you…"

"You took off your wedding band for me?"

"No, I took it off for me. And for my girls. They need me to move on with my life, because they're growing up, becoming individuals who need more than a father who stopped his life years ago. And I need me to get past this because it's time. That one I give you the credit for. You've made me get involved again, made me aware of my girls in new ways."

"I thought it must have been very difficult for you. Especially since you have the girls there every day to remind you of the things you wanted in your life, things that you'll never have."

He took hold of her hand, but not to hold it so much as to caress it. To rub his thumb over the sensitive mound beneath her thumb and massage the areas above with his forefinger. Slow, gentle swirls tracing from side to side, moving up to her knuckles, exploring each one with delicacy and such skill…surgeon's hands. Then he explored her fingers, one by one, starting at the base and with his thumb and first two fingers, moving to the tip, stroking gently, over and over. Each finger. Again and again.

By the time Eric finally took hold of her whole hand, she was as seduced as if he'd made passionate love to her, as sated as she'd ever known she could be. All that from only a touch. The jolt of it sizzling all the way down to her toes. As he took a firmer grip, her toes curled, and the muscles in her legs tightened. She wanted to be seduced. Oh, how she wanted to be seduced. But she wasn't sure that was Eric's intent. "If we do spend the night here I have candy bars," she said, her voice in a wobbly whisper. Of all the silly things anyone could possibly say at a moment like that, here she was, babbling on about candy bars. "And crackers with peanut butter. Bottles of water, a flashlight, a lighter, which I have to take good care of because it belongs to—"

"You'd flunk my course," he said, his voice in low harmony with the night sounds of the forest. Seductive, full of suggestion. Primal.

"Your course?"

"Wilderness survival." He leaned over and kissed her on the jaw. "I'm a very good instructor."

"Are you sure about this?" she asked as ribbons of moonlight flowing played wickedly with him…casting him in a half-hidden aura that was so seductive she had to force herself to breathe. Was she ready for this? Was Eric ready? Last time they'd saved a patient together they'd come together in a kiss. But this time a kiss wouldn't be enough.

"I have rules, Dinah. They've governed everything I am, everything I do, for such a long time."

"Do you want to break them?" It was a hopeful question, but she feared the answer, because even if he did want to break *his* rules, she still wasn't sure she could, or would, break her own.

It was a dangerous line they were walking now, skirting the obvious, so close to toppling over. Afraid of what would happen when they did. Or if they didn't.

"I loved my wife, Dinah. It was a good marriage. No problems. Patricia was everything I'd ever wanted and she made me happy beyond belief. Sometimes, when I go home from work, I still expect to find her there. Except I've had as many years without her now as I had with her. And I wonder if I want to be stuck where I am, if it's a subconscious choice or if something else is stopping me from moving forward. I mean, right now *we* should be naked together. Wrapped up in your blanket, getting warm from each other's body heat. But here I am, talking about my wife. Make no mistake, though, I really want to get naked with you."

"Maybe it's not the right time for us. It happens. The right people meet at the wrong time. I mean, I came to White Elk set on spending this part of my life being alone and trying to figure out all the mistakes I've made in the other parts of my life so I don't make them again. Getting naked in the forest with a handsome doctor was nowhere in those plans, not even at the bottom of the list." Although had there been a real list, being naked with Eric anywhere would have been climbing its way to the top at this very moment.

"But what if it's the right time, and we're so dead set on being resistant that we don't see it?"

"Ah, yes, breaking down the barriers. Sometimes the hardest ones to destroy are the ones we can't see."

"Are you threatened by my feelings for Patricia?"

"Not threatened. I like knowing how passionate you were about her. It tells me what kind of man you are." The kind she'd never been lucky enough to find. *Until now.* Although she did worry some that if she let herself get involved with Eric, Eric might not let himself get involved with her. Not in the way she needed. It wasn't his fault, and it wasn't even necessarily something she wanted to discuss with him because, as of this very moment, they weren't involved. Flirting with the idea, yes. Doing the deed...she simply didn't know if that could ever be a reality for them.

"So what do we do?" he asked. "Right now, when any man in his right mind would be seducing this beautiful woman rather than sitting here on the river bank listing all the reasons why he's not, what should we do?"

"Start over. Take it a step at a time, with no expectations." But full of realization.

Eric pulled off her bandanna and ran his fingers through her tangled hair. "Well, then, beautiful stranger, my name is Eric Ramsey, and I'm quite capable of rescuing a fair damsel lost in the woods should the need arise."

"And I'm Dinah Corday, lost in so many ways, who would welcome a rescue should the need arise." She took his hand in hers and felt the immediate sensation between them. A spark, or maybe a sparkle. Or maybe an illumination as bright as the stars above.

"How will I know when the need arises?"

"It's arising," she said, her voice as tranquil as the rustling leaves on the trees surrounding them. Sliding her hand up his arm, she liked the feel of it. Strong arm. Lean. Well-muscled, and larger than her grasp around it. Was she causing goosebumps on him somewhere the way merely the feel of his arm was causing them on her? "I'm not an old-fashioned girl, Eric. My life may have suited me better had I been, but there are only so many moments given us for the things in which we find pleasure, and we waste too many of them." No, she was not old-fashioned, but not smart in love, either. Yet this wasn't love, she was telling herself hard and fast as her fingers refused to cease their journey over his flesh. Not love. Not love. Couldn't be. She wouldn't let it be.

He chuckled, the rumble of it resonant in his chest. "There's no way I ever had that impression of you."

"And that's good?" Suddenly she wasn't sure why she was being so bold. Did she want to be seduced by him? Or to seduce him? Silly questions. Of course she did. She had almost from the moment he'd left her standing in the rain with his umbrella while he'd driven off.

"It is, if you've got that blanket you said you did."

"I had a pillow, but it went with Shawn," she added, reluctantly letting go of his arm so she could pick up her backpack. If ever there'd been a time when she didn't want to lose the feel of flesh to flesh, this was it, for she feared that in the mere seconds it would take to unzip the pack and pull out the blanket, he would change his mind.

Or she would lose her nerve.

"What I have in mind doesn't require a pillow."

After she'd pulled the blanket from the backpack, she saw exactly what Eric had in mind. Somewhere in the urgent tumble of shedding clothes and exploration so frantic that it promised to explode, the blanket was totally forgotten, and the pile of discarded clothes on the bed of pine needles was enough. They were naked and entangled, the night was chilly, and neither one of them noticed anything but each other while the natural heat of so many emerging emotions cocooned them in a fire that wasn't even touched by the raw elements surrounding them.

"Are *you* sure?" he asked, much more quickly that he'd anticipated. More quickly than he'd wanted. He'd come prepared, and debated whether or not he should. Debated whether or not he could go through with this, of if guilt would pull him away from her. But now…

"We don't have to," she whispered, sensing his apprehension.

"Yes," he choked, "we do."

"Then I'm sure…"

He responded with a guttural moan then plunged deep and hard, bringing her to an immediate climax that coaxed him to his own. To start with the final act the way they did… Dinah liked that. She also liked that afterwards they spent their leisure pleasuring each other with the less urgent things that came of lovers taking their time to get to know each other. The little pleasures, the little discoveries. It was nice….nicer than she'd ever dreamed this could be. She craved the slow exploration of his hand on her, craved the building of a trust she'd never thought she could have. Because here, with Eric, she was vulnerable and trusting. And for the first time in her life, it didn't frighten her. It's exactly what she wanted to be—with him, and for him.

CHAPTER SEVEN

ANOTHER blanket would have been nice, but they were wrapped so tightly in each other that it didn't matter. Nothing about them was cold. And everything was perfect. His body matched hers, inch for inch, in a hard press. Sensually, though. Not sexually. He felt good, squeezed tight to her, pulling her into his contours. She felt the way a woman should feel with a man so close to her they were practically sharing one heartbeat. "I've never done…*this* outside," she whispered, as the kisses he was trailing down her neck threatened to rob her of breath. The chill of the sensation radiated all the way down to her kneecaps, tiny little prickles of pleasure with every kiss.

"Neither have I," he said, breaking a perfect cadence just long enough to start a new journey from her neck down to her breasts. "But I think it's already become my favorite thing to do in the great outdoors."

"Are you going to add this to your wilderness survival course?" she gasped, as he teased her nipple with his tongue first, then his teeth. She arched to him, wanting more.

He didn't stop long enough to answer. Rather, he mumbled a very rough "Uh-uh" as his hand came up to claim the breast his mouth hadn't yet claimed.

In the distance she heard the call of a night bird…was he courting his lady love? Or was he alone, looking for a lady to love? It was a sad, mournful call, one she knew so well in her heart. One that had temporarily fled from her.

"What was that sigh?" he asked, finally pulling back a little.

"Just thinking what tonight would have been like if we'd gone back to town."

"Are you glad we didn't?"

"Very glad," she whispered, words murmured as his lips claimed hers full and hard.

The kiss was so hard and full of long-held passion that she feared her lips would bruise, or that she would bruise Eric's lips. But as what couldn't possibly intensify did just that, and as she felt the deep probing of his tongue, and returned it, she kicked off that single blanket and rolled over until they were side to side. Then she pulled back enough so she could see his face. His beautiful face.

"What are you doing?" he asked.

"Just looking."

"But it's dark, there's not really much to see."

He was wrong, though. There was everything to see, and it made no matter that there wasn't sufficient light. For she saw it in her heart. And it frightened her, because she wanted it so badly.

But this wasn't love. Wasn't love. Couldn't be love.

Could it?

"There's always something to see." Sliding her leg across his hip, she wiggled closer, pressed her lips to his ear. "If you know what you're looking for."

What she was doing to him, in the explicit moves, in the subtleties. As he rolled on top of her, so ready to take her again, it was clear that this second time would be as fast as the first. There was no subtlety in what he needed or what she wanted. "Do you know what you're looking for?" he practically groaned.

"I think I do." In the perfect spot underneath him, finding the perfect rhythm with him… "I think I really do." Though knowing and truly having were so far apart.

"Eric, do you read me?"

The crackling noise from the walkie-talkie startled her awake, and at first blink Dinah was surprised to find that she was totally naked underneath the blanket. At second blink, she was surprised to find she was totally alone.

"Come in, Eric."

It was Neil's voice. She recognized it.

"Come in, Eric. Can you hear me?"

Rolling over on her belly, suddenly very self-conscious about her condition, she grabbed the walkie-talkie from atop her backpack. "Eric's not here right now," she said, struggling to sit up and keep the blanket wrapped tight.

"Tell him that the Dawsons are all stable. Everything's fine here, and we were wondering when the two of you were going to head back. We don't need to send a rescue team out to find you, do we?"

Even though Neil was chuckling at the suggestion, Dinah felt totally humiliated.

"We can have a helicopter out there to get you in the next ten minutes. Unless you care to camp out there a little longer."

"Ten minutes is fine," she said, trying not to sound as despondent as she felt. Had it been that bad for Eric? Was he having morning-after regrets? Was he still battling over his feelings about his wife, and now feeling guilty about what they'd done? She felt horrible about that. Didn't want to cause him any pain. But she was afraid that's what she'd done.

"Seriously?"

"Seriously. I'm not sure Eric will want the ride, but I do." He'd said he had rules. She'd known her own rules. And broken them. Another case of her emotions ruling her head. "And I'll be ready."

"Then ten minutes it is."

Well, it was something she couldn't fight. Something she *wouldn't* fight. And maybe it was good to find out now, before they…what? Got too serious?

Dinah sighed, tugging on her clothes. Eric had to be in the throes of complete emotional regret. "But I knew," she said, slinging her backpack over her shoulder, getting ready to hike on down the trail to the pick-up point. If she met up with Eric somewhere along the way, she'd simply pretend that last night hadn't happened. That would make it easier for him. Ignore the deed and soon the fact of it would be forgotten.

Except she wouldn't forget. She'd expected… well, it didn't matter what she'd expected, did it? It was what it was. She should have known better. Nothing was going to change.

As it turned out, Eric wasn't too far off from the campsite, which surprised her. He hadn't gone off and left her at all, which was what she'd thought he'd done. In fact, he was sitting on a rock, staring out over the river, mere yards from where they'd slept. In sight all along. Yet so far away in the things that mattered.

He had to get back to her. She'd be waking up soon, wondering where he was. Then she'd be jumping to the wrong conclusion. Well, not exactly the wrong conclusion because when he'd opened his eyes that morning, he'd wanted to feel guilty, wanted to feel disloyal. But all he'd felt was good…good in a way he hadn't felt in such a long time. That's what had sent him off to be alone, to think. Because his feelings scared him. The fact that he *had* feelings after so many years scared him even more.

Oh, he'd been accused of hiding—behind his job, behind his daughters, behind his sister. Too many times one woman or another had approached him, shown interest, tried being friendly only to have him brush them off when their overtures proved more than he'd wanted from them. But that's what had always made it easier for him, what had always made it better. He had excuses. Places to hide. Safety in a life he really didn't belong in.

But Patricia wouldn't have wanted this. She would have wanted him to be happy, to get on with his life, find someone else, be normal again. In theory, it sounded easy. In practice, it was so damned hard because it wasn't in the plan. His life had been set the way he'd wanted it, everything laid out. Perfect. Then she'd died and left him floundering. What to do without her? What to do with the girls?

Honestly, it had been easier just sticking to the original plan—the original plan minus Patricia. Except easier was getting so frustrating lately because he wanted…needed a new life. Being with Dinah made him see what he wanted in that life and, logically, he should have been feeling guilty. But he wasn't. And it hurt, letting Patricia slip away. He wasn't guilty, though. Just reconciling. And sad.

Dinah made things better. Made them good. Changed everything. Yet she was running away from him as hard and fast as she could. She'd take a few steps closer then bolt. One night brought them closer, but didn't bring them together. The thing was, being together scared him, too. So maybe he was running away as hard as she was, and hadn't even realized it. Or why wasn't he waking up with her right now, making sweet morning love to her the way he should have been?

Sitting on a boulder jutting out over the river, with the early sun beginning to shine down on his shoulders, Eric watched the water flow by. It moved along no matter what happened, the way his life should have. But his life had been stagnant for so long, sitting in a little dammed-up pool off to the side, flowing nowhere. Until Dinah. "Dinah…" he murmured. He didn't want to hurt her. If ever there was a woman he could love again, she was the one. So unlike Patricia in just about every way, she attracted him like he'd never expected anyone could again. And it was a different feeling of attraction, something so unexpected. With Patricia it had been calm, steady, all about a sense of well-being. With Dinah it was wild, crazy, off balance. And, God help him, he wanted that in his life. But was it fair to Dinah when he wasn't sure if he could get to the place where it was truly good with him…good without all these doubts in himself? She deserved more.

Eric stood, stretched, and looked around him. In the distance he could hear the sound of an approaching helicopter, and wondered if Neil had sent someone to get them. A brisk morning hike would have been good. Very cathartic, and very long. Almost three hours from here. So maybe a short ride was best. Time to get back to reality and see what happened next. Maybe he needed some distance from Dinah…just until he was sure he wouldn't hurt her, just until he was sure about…himself.

Dinah…Thinking about her brought a smile to his face, and quickened his step as he hiked back to the spot where they'd spent the night. But halfway there, he met up with her, and even though he'd expected her to come at him with a vengeance for leaving her alone, even though she had never really been out of his sight, she simply looked up at him. "Our ride's here," she said. "I decided I didn't want to hike out this morning."

She was avoiding the obvious, but he saw it in her eyes. The questions, the doubts. She couldn't hide it. She couldn't hide anything from him, and it unnerved him, being so aware of her. "It's not easy yet, Dinah. Whatever this is going on between us…it's not going to be easy. We're both still fighting against it and I needed a few minutes to think. That's the only reason I went off by myself."

"I understand," she said.

But she didn't. She doubted him, and he saw that in her, too. It killed him that such a little thing had hurt her because he didn't want Dinah hurt by anything, most of all by him. "I didn't leave you, Dinah. I don't want you thinking that I did."

"People leave. It's not a big deal. They leave, you move on."

"But I didn't leave."

"And I *said* I understand. So let's just get in the helicopter and get back, OK? I have a shift at the hospital this morning, and I have to cook this evening."

Well, she'd shut the door. Shut it and locked it up tight and he didn't know how to open it. He wanted to be optimistic about their future together, but he wasn't sure he knew *how* to be optimistic anymore. For Dinah, though, he really did want to be.

"I'm glad you saved all of them," Janice said, then immediately turned Eric's daughters loose on him.

"I called the hospital in Salt Lake on the way in and they told me that Shawn is in surgery, his father is in Intensive Care and Troy is waking up, doing better than expected. I wish all our rescues could turn out that well."

Now that he was back, Pippa and Paige were going wild, holding on to him, trying to out-talk each other, telling him all the little details of their night without him. "They don't know what he does, do they?" Dinah asked Janice.

"They know he's a doctor, and that he helps make people feel better."

"But they don't know about the rescues?"

"He thinks they're too young to understand. He's afraid they'd be worried, especially as they don't have a mother."

Dinah dropped to her knees in the grass then sprawled out. She wasn't physically tired so much as she was emotionally worn out. Too much had happened, too much to think about, and she just wanted to stay there in the grass for a while, empty her mind and stare up at the sky.

"By the way, I have a message from Angela," Janice said, standing over her, looking down.

Dinah opened her eyes. "She's OK, isn't she?"

"Fine. Perfect."

"Not in labor?"

Janice shook her head. Then smiled. "But she said to tell you that she named her new daughter after your grandmother."

Dinah bolted straight to her feet. "She had her baby? When? Why didn't someone call me? Is she in the hospital? Is the baby OK? Who delivered the baby? Did Gabby get here, or did—?"

"Whoa," Janice said, thrusting out her hand to

stop the outpouring of questions. "Everybody's fine. Angela is in the hospital, and she wouldn't let anybody tell you because she knew you'd come back to her in the middle of the night, and she thought that was too dangerous. So everyone here had to promise…"

"Neil knew?"

Janice nodded. "That's why he offered the helicopter to get you back here."

"And Eric?"

"Not Eric. He'd have tried getting you back here in the middle of the night, and we decided it was better for him to rest."

"I can't believe no one said a word to me."

"Your sister's request."

"But she's OK? You wouldn't be keeping something from me, would you?"

"Other than the fact that it's a girl, her name is Sarah, she weighs seven pounds, and she's beautiful, there's really nothing else to tell you except that Angela wants to see you as soon as you can get there."

As soon as she could get to the hospital turned into about fifteen minutes, as Dinah bypassed her room, a shower and a good meal at the lodge.

She hopped in her car, drove straight to the hospital, parked in the no-parking zone at the front and ran in the door, fully aware that she looked like she'd spent a night on the mountain.

On the way to the maternity ward, she paused to look at the babies in the nursery. Three of them. All beautiful, all of them causing a lump to form in her throat. The one on the left was her niece, as it turned out. Naturally, that was the baby she'd already picked as the prettiest. Of course, she'd never met a baby that wasn't beautiful but as it so happened, little Sarah was the one who brought tears to her eyes.

As the nurse held her up for Dinah to get a better look, a lifetime of possibilities for Sarah passed before her eyes…dance lessons, school plays, girlfriends, pretty dresses, boyfriends, first date, first kiss… First longing, and it was hers. To have a baby of her own. She'd subjugated that desire for so long then with Charles she'd thought about it again. Except after he'd given her the diamond ring he'd also given her the news that he'd had a vasectomy years ago to avoid the possibility of children. He would treat them as patients but he didn't want them interfering in his real life.

She'd been disappointed. Told him so, and asked him to reconsider. Maybe they could adopt? Or he could have a vasectomy reversal. He did reconsider, but not about having children. That's when he'd started to reconsider whether or not he wanted her. And she'd started to reconsider whether or not she wanted him.

But now...*this* was what she wanted. It was like her biological clock had reserved all its ticking for this very moment, and now it was ticking like crazy. She wanted a baby of her own. Wanted that joy Angela had. Wanted that feeling of complete fulfillment. It's what made sense to her more than anything else.

"She's a real looker," Eric said, stepping up behind her. "Even though she hasn't got any hair yet, I think she's going to be a redhead like her aunt." He slipped his arm around Dinah's waist and she melted against him. Quite a pair they were, dirty, tired, bruised and scratched, and standing in the hall smiling at the babies. "I remember the first time I saw the twins...I couldn't believe how perfect they were. Perfect fingers and toes, perfect little eyes and noses..."

"It puts everything into proper perspective, doesn't it? Makes you truly believe all's right with the world."

"All is right with the world…their world. And that's the way it should be."

"And then they have to grow up," she said on a wistful sigh.

"Like I said before, you'll be a good mother, Dinah."

"My life is too up and down to drag a baby into it right now." But in the future? Admittedly, she could almost see that happening, with Eric. Thinking with her heart again.

"Only if you want it to be up and down."

"That's not what I want, but so far it hasn't been under my control." Spinning away, Dinah headed off in the direction of her sister's room, half expecting Eric to follow, but when she didn't hear the clicking of his heels on the tile floor, she decided it was for the best. Being around him almost made her believe she could have it all. *Almost.*

"Well, I see you fixed yourself up for the occasion," Angela said. She was sitting up in bed, looking happier than Dinah had ever seen her look. Positively glowing.

"I slept on pine needles," she said, plucking one from her hair. "Climbed down a rock. Waded in an icy cold river." And made love like she'd never known it could be. But that didn't show on her, and she was going to take care that it wouldn't.

"And you look radiant. I heard the father and both the boys are going to make it."

"Why didn't you let somebody call me?" Dinah asked, pulling up a chair and sitting down next to her sister.

"Because you were needed out there, and I was fine here. Brad's mother and sister flew in. And Gabby got here in time to do the delivery, so I had a veritable force of strong women here to help me through, when you take into account that half the women in White Elk stopped by because they knew you were out on the rescue and thought I might need a birth coach."

"She's beautiful, Angela. Sarah is so beautiful, and amazing.

"Then you've seen her?"

"We came to an understanding about her first date, and her first kiss, and her wedding dress."

Angela laughed. "Sounds to me like you might have a few mommy dreams going on of your own. So, did something happen out there in the woods you want to tell me about?"

"Nothing that matters," Dinah said, trying to sound less wistful than she felt. "It was…difficult."

"The rescue, or what came after?"

"Both. Eric and I, we…we got closer, I think. But it scares me. I know I trust him, with all my heart. But I get too emotional, make bad decisions…"

"And you think Eric might be a bad decision?"

"No. But I think he might be a wrong decision, at least right now. He's still got…"

"Patricia?"

Dinah nodded. "And it feels like I'm pushing him away from her."

"Is he ready to be pushed?"

"That's the thing. He might be. But maybe he's just responding to, well…you know."

Angela grinned. "So it was a nice night in the forest after all?"

Dinah grinned back. "It was, and that's what scared me. I think we should have waited. I mean, it wasn't that long ago that he took off his wedding ring, and now…" She shrugged. "I don't want to make a mess of this, and I don't want to hurt him. But I think I'm doing both."

"Then maybe he's the one you should be talking to."

Sighing, Dinah pulled another pine needle from her hair. "Maybe I will. Anyway, let's talk about you now. Like, if Brad's mother is here, what about Brad? Have you talked to him?"

"Briefly. Nothing's changed. He didn't even want to know if I had a boy or girl. But his mother and sister have had it with Brad, and they want to be part of Sarah's life. Begged me to let them be a part of it."

"Are you going to let them?"

"How can I not? They love her. What Brad's done is his choice, but I'm not going to punish the people in his family who love Sarah because he doesn't."

"It's his loss, and he doesn't even know it." Dinah smiled at her younger sister. "You're going to be a fantastic mom, you know that?"

"I'd be even better if you'd consider settling down here in White Elk with Sarah and me. Give it some serious thought, Dinah. I know this situation with Eric is up in the air, but you don't have a real home. Mom travels all the time so it wouldn't make sense to live near her since she's never in the same place more than a month or two. Which leaves your favorite sister and your favorite niece, both of whom really want you here. I intend on raising my daughter right here, and I really, *really* want you to be part of our lives. Janice was telling me how good you've been with Eric's daughters, and I want that for my daughter…from her aunt."

Settling down… It sounded so good. Sounded good when Angela initially asked, and sounded good an hour later, as Dinah was letting the warm spray from the shower slide down her tired, aching body. It still sounded good thirty minutes after that, on her way back to the hospital to cover half a shift.

But sounding good didn't mean it was going to be simple. And what she and Eric had started…that didn't make it any easier.

Had they really started something? She wondered. Pondered. Remembered. Fantasized. She was trying not to feel so contented about it, but she was contented. There was no denying it. She was totally contented and it scared her to death because she still didn't believe that the kind of contentment she was feeling could come without pitfalls. She wanted to believe, and Eric made her come close to believing, but she was still on the edge of that ledge, looking down, not sure whether to take the leap or not. And this time she didn't have Eric there to encourage her. It was her leap to take on her own. Probably the biggest leap she would ever take in her life. If she took it at all.

CHAPTER EIGHT

"I WANT those!" Pippa squealed as the three of them passed the lodge's gift shop. This was girls' day out for Paige, Pippa and Dinah, and right now Pippa was practically jumping up and down over the prospect of buying pink shoelaces. Shoelaces like the ones Dinah had used to leave a trail for Eric.

"Did your daddy tell you about the shoelaces?" Dinah asked, wondering how much Eric had said about their rescue. Or, specifically, about her.

"He said you acted like a girl," Paige volunteered.

"And what's wrong with acting like a girl?" Dinah asked, smiling. "Did your daddy tell you what's wrong with acting like a girl?"

"He said it's very good, that he likes it. Did you and Daddy have a picnic? Is that why you were in the woods?" Paige asked.

Picnic wasn't quite the word to describe what they'd had. In fact, there wasn't a word to describe it. Wasn't a word to describe the way she was feeling because of it either. Happy. Excited. Scared. It was a jumble of mixed emotions, and she was a jumble of mixed confusions because there'd been no aftermath. No mention. No overtures. No nothing.

Two days later, it was like nothing had happened between them. They'd worked a couple of shifts together at the hospital, stayed strictly professional about it, and…nothing. Eric had gone his way, she'd gone hers. No knowing winks. No suggestive smiles. Cordial nods, for heaven's sake! "Yes, we definitely had a picnic," she explained, trying to shake off the gloomy mood trying to slip down over her, trying to remind herself that Eric's feelings toward his wife most likely had everything to do with what was happening between them now. She understood it, sympathized. Told herself it was for the best since she wasn't looking for any kind of a real commitment. Of course, for just a little while…a moment in time, she'd thought that maybe… "So, are you two ladies ready for high tea?"

Pippa looked longingly at the pink shoelaces in the gift-shop window as Dinah hurried the girls off to the conservatory and left them there for a few minutes in Redmond's capable hands while she went to the kitchen to check on the progress of the evening meal prep. As it turned out, everything was under control. Her staff was busy chopping, dicing, slicing… Unfortunately, knowing she supervised a well-run kitchen didn't give her the feeling of accomplishment she longed for. In fact, she wondered why she was still in White Elk. Angela was surrounded by women fussing over her and the baby, the kitchen was well managed by Angela's support staff and the ambitious, if not ubiquitous Oswaldo. All in all, her presence in White Elk was almost superfluous. She'd come because she'd been needed but, as it had turned out, nobody here really needed her.

Just when she'd thought she might stay, it seemed like it could be time to go. Because certainly, she couldn't face Eric day after day, if she caused him any discomfort. He had his life here, his work, his family. She had…a few hopes, maybe the makings of a dream.

"How do we look?" Pippa and Paige asked in unison as Dinah entered the conservatory a few minutes later. They were in pink floral dresses, identical, and one of the servers had given them matching hats. Grinning, giggling, blowing kisses into the air, they were capturing the attention of all the people there to partake of high tea.

"Fabulous," she said, responding with a curtsey to each girl. If she did leave White Elk, saying goodbye to these girls would be one of the hardest things she'd have to do. It was amazing how much she'd come to love them in such a short time. "Absolutely stunning and beautiful."

The girls grinned from ear to ear then Pippa stepped forward and motioned for Dinah to bend down. "We can have finger sandwiches or ladyfingers with our tea," she whispered, "but we don't want *fingers*." She held up her hand and wiggled her own fingers for Dinah to see. "Can we go somewhere else and have ice cream?"

"You know you're not supposed to ask," Paige reminded her. "Daddy said so. It's not polite."

"But how are you supposed to get what you want if you don't ask for it?" Pippa argued. "And I want ice cream, not fingers. That's why I asked."

Sound reasoning in a five-year-old's mind, Dinah thought, but the differences in their personalities were coming out in a big way, and it was interesting to see. Pippa had absolutely no trouble going after what she wanted, while Paige was more thoughtful about it, trying to abide by the rules more than her sister did. Even if those rules did stipulate they had to eat *fingers*.

Eric was going to have himself a handful in the years to come. Lucky man because his girls adored him. And lucky girls because they were adored by their father. "I'll talk to Estelle, the woman in charge of the tea, and I think she can probably find you ice cream. But so you'll know, finger sandwiches don't have real fingers in them. Usually, it's something like a cream cheese spread or cucumber. And lady fingers are simply cakes. They're called fingers because they're about the size of a finger."

The girls regarded each other for a moment, settling on an unspoken agreement. "Ice cream," they both said. Something in their expressions said they were staying on the safe side.

Tea was nice. They talked, the girls chattered on and on about the things they liked to do—

swimming, playing video games, watching movies, going for walks. They wanted riding lessons, wanted ballet lessons, wanted new bicycles…all normal things. And it was so fun being involved in all that. As the hour progressed, they made plans for more shopping trips, another high tea and a talk with White Elk's resident ballet teacher…although Dinah did tell them it was all subject to their father's approval.

She liked their inquisitiveness. Hoped that if she ever had children of her own they'd be just like these two. Children of her own…a thought that had come to mind so much lately. Especially when she held her brand-new niece, Sarah. Foolish thought for someone who seemed to be heading toward the exit.

Trying to wipe out all thoughts of the things that *weren't* happening in her life, like babies and twin daughters and relationships, Dinah took each girl by the hand after tea was over and led them down the hall to the gift shop, then bought them pink shoelaces. Why not? It was fun indulging them, and for all their exuberance, and their long wish list, these little girls were not spoiled. They were a delight, two people she loved spending time with. Two girls so much alike they were practically the same, except they weren't. She could see the differences more and more all the time—differences that would be more noticeable to a woman…to their mother.

There were times, like today at high tea, watching Pippa and Paige charm every last person in the conservatory, that she could see herself being their mother. It wasn't a fantasy, wasn't even a fond wish, because with that wish, by necessity, would come Eric. Yet if a woman were afforded the opportunity to hand-pick the children she'd want to have as daughters, she couldn't see herself picking children other than Pippa and Paige. They were well adjusted, well behaved, smart. A true extension of their father.

And of their mother. That was something she couldn't forget because that, she feared, was the final stumbling block to any kind of relationship she and Eric might have had. Maybe, just maybe he couldn't see her as mother to his children. Good as their playmate or babysitter, but not their mother.

Too emotional to be a good nurse, according to Charles. Too emotional to be a good mother, according to Eric?

Or maybe just not the right mother... She sighed on that discouraging note. If he was finally getting past Patricia as his wife, but not *her* as the girls' mother...well, that was something no one could deal with. Not her. Not even Eric.

"You look rested," Eric commented. Offhand comment, one he'd make to anyone, in a tone of voice he'd use on anyone.

"I'm fine," she said, shutting his office door. "Look, Eric, we need to talk."

He set aside the patient chart he'd been reading. "About the girls?"

"The girls are wonderful. We had a lovely time at high tea this afternoon, and unless you don't want me involved with them, we've made plans for a few more outings while I'm still here."

"Still here?"

"In White Elk. I just tendered my resignation here at the hospital. Pending finding someone to replace me. I won't leave you in a bind."

"Where the hell did this come from?" he snapped.

"I'd never planned on staying. I was here to help my sister, and she's being overrun with help with the baby now, her kitchen's in good order, and there's no reason for me to stay. I've been thinking about going to Costa Rica for a while… I know someone there who operates a small resort and there's an opening in the kitchen for a sous chef."

"A sous chef?"

He was being too calm. She could see the explosion about to erupt. His mouth was drawn into a thin line, his eyes narrowing. The thing was, she couldn't interpret his anger. And maybe she didn't want to. "It's a good job, nice area. I'll have my own little cottage…"

"That's what you want? Your own little cottage?"

"It's a good opportunity." And he wasn't asking her to stay. Somewhere in her plan for this conversation, she'd envisioned the version where he'd pulled her into his arms and asked her to stay. "Good salary, wonderful climate."

"Oh, so you want a little cottage *and* a nice climate?" Words spoken harshly.

"What I want, Eric, is a life. In case you haven't noticed, the one I'm living right now is pretty much bits and pieces of other people's lives. I work a hospital shift here and there at your pleasure, cook at my sister's pleasure. The only thing I do that could be remotely construed as my own life is what I do with Paige and Pippa. So if a little cottage and a nice climate are what it takes to get me closer to having a life of my own, that's what I'm going to do." Even if it broke her heart.

"And what happens to Paige and Pippa when you leave?" he asked, his anger rippling even closer to the surface. "What happens when they come to look forward to ladies' day out, and you're gone?"

"Then you can have a daddy day with them every week. So long as you do little-girl things with them. Because they need that, Eric. I mean, you should have seen them at high tea with their hats and pretty dresses, having so much fun."

"I don't do high tea."

Unequivocal, flat response. He didn't intend on budging one inch in his position. "Or pink shoe-laces?" she asked, bending down over the desk so he couldn't ignore her the way he was trying hard to do. "Because they are little girls who need little-girls things like pink shoelaces."

He cleared his throat. Pushed back in his chair, pushed his chair back. "If they want pink, I can buy them pink."

Well, his intent was clear, and she had no place
in it. Any delusions of staying had been wiped
away now. He'd had his opening, his chance to
ask her to stay. Even a hint at wanting her to
stay...for him...would have been enough. But
he was hiding behind Paige and Pippa now.
Which meant Eric considered her, and what
they'd done, a mistake. He didn't want to deal
with her. She made him nervous. Reminded him
of things he didn't want to be reminded of, things
he didn't want to leave behind. And there was no
way to fight it. Not that she would. Eric had
every right to his feelings.

And she had every right to hers. Well, at least
now she knew. This was probably for the best,
she decided. What had happened with Eric...
she'd never done anything like that before. Never
just jumped into anything so quickly, so inti-
mately and spontaneously as she had with him.
But what was the point of getting involved only
up to a point? Which was what their involvement
would have been—only up to a point. So it was
good she knew. The best thing. She understood
Eric's regrets, his confusion. Yet, still, she'd
hoped...

But it hurt. She wouldn't deny it. Knowing came with a fair sting to it.

"Look, do you still want me working my shift? Like I said, I've agreed to keep working here until you can find someone to replace me," Dinah said, struggling to keep the wilting emotion from her voice. "But if you'd rather not keep me around…"

"Why wouldn't I want you working your shift? And where the hell did you ever get the idea I didn't want you working here anymore?"

"Well, for starters, what happened that night in the woods…"

He backed away from her even more. "Has nothing to do with you being here."

"Sure, it does. I mean, look at you now. You can barely be in the same room with me. How can that make for a good working relationship, even if it's only for a few more days, until you replace me?"

He dropped his head back on his chair, drew in a deep breath, and shut his eyes. "Damn," he muttered, nearly under his breath. "I don't want you to leave."

"But you don't want me staying, either, do you?"

"I don't know what I want. But it's not about you, Dinah." He opened his eyes. "And I'm sorry that's the way it seems. I'm just…"

"Look, let me make this easy for you, OK? I'll leave then you don't have to deal with…me. I know it's not easy for you, Eric." She glanced at the picture of Patricia on his desk. Beautiful woman. Bright eyes, warm smile. The woman Eric loved. "I understand that, and I don't want to make things more difficult for you."

"Costa Rica makes them more difficult for me."

"But Costa Rica makes things easier for me. I get…involved, Eric. I can't help myself. That's just me, though. I can't detach myself, put the various aspects of my life into individual compartments the way you seem to do. It would be good if I could, because I wouldn't end up doing so many dumb things, like falling for the wrong man."

"Falling for the wrong man?"

"You know that's my history. I haven't kept any secrets about that."

"So when you say *falling*, what, exactly, do you mean?"

"You know, *falling*…spending time with, enjoying the company of, wanting more time with." Making love with more than one night. "That's all." No mention of love intended.

"Look, Dinah, I know we haven't had much time to ourselves, but—"

"No time to ourselves, Eric? *No time?*" That was his choice, and maybe it was a good choice since she'd gone and done it again—fallen for the wrong man, love possibly intended. "But that's fine. I'll stay out of your way while I'm still here, and in another week or so, you won't even have to worry about that." She glanced at Patricia's picture again and thought about Eric. Maybe someday, someone would have that same kind of enduring love for her.

"Stay out of my way? Where did you ever get the idea that I want you to stay out of my way?" He pushed himself from his desk chair, and started to round the desk, but this time Dinah was the one who backed away from him.

"That's what you've been doing, isn't it? And I understand, Eric. I totally understand."

"Good, then maybe you can explain it to me because it's driving me crazy. I mean, all I can think about is that night in the woods, and when I let those thoughts distract me, I might as well hang up the white coat because I'm no good to anyone. Which isn't what my patients need from me. If anything, my preference would be to have you in my way as much as I can."

"I distract you?" she asked, still backing away as he came toward her. Backing, but in smaller steps now as his steps toward her grew larger.

"What did you think? That I'd make love to you once, and that was it?"

"Maybe. Since that's the way it was, and you've barely even spoken to me since." Her back to the wall next to his office door, she had two choices. Stay where she was, pressed into the bookshelf on her right, or scoot to the left and slip out into the hall. "I don't make good decisions, Eric. I've told you…"

"And you don't think I'm a good decision?"

"That's not what I meant."

He clicked the lock on the door. "It's not what I expected, Dinah. None of it is and I'm trying to sort things out. Trying to let go, and hang on, and change and adjust. And that's why I've been avoiding you. The only reason." In the next instant she was locked in his embrace, their lips together. Urgent. Hungry. His fingers pressing down the sides of her spine better than the feel of any fingers on her, ever.

She arched against him, felt the hard outline of his erection on her pelvis and rocked herself into it. Craving it. Craving him, as his hands moved forward, pulled up the green cotton scrub top she was wearing and sought her breasts. Even through the thin silk of her bra, the feel of his hands cupping her, exploring her made her want more, lust for more. Give more of herself to him.

Eric groaned as her tongue sought his, sucked his, and he groaned even louder while she yanked his scrub shirt loose from his pants and ran her hands over his belly, up his chest, twining her fingers in the mat of soft chest hair, flicking his nipple, squeezing, teasing… It was only when her fingers returned to his belly and were frantically engaged in untying the drawstring to his scrub pants that she caught herself. "We should probably get a room if we want to do this," she said, her voice so rough with want she didn't recognize it.

Her words were the bucket of cold water they needed, because Eric stepped back, shuddered, ran his hand through his hair then let out a final groan. "You make me want to do things I've never done," he admitted.

"Is that good?" Her immediate fear was that he felt conflicted, or guilty. It was always the big wall between them. The thing she always feared. And she couldn't argue or compete with that. "Or bad?"

A smile crept to his face. A deliciously sexy smile on his lips that eventually spread to his eyes. "Very good." He opened his arms to her, and she practically fell into them. "I'm not sure what we're going to do, at least in the long term, and I'm positive of what we'd do in the short term if we let ourselves. Which leaves us in between, doesn't it?"

"In between isn't bad," she said. In fact, it felt very good. Everything she'd hoped for. Of course, she didn't hope in the long term, which was what made the in between what it was. Perfect, for now. "Is it?"

Eric didn't answer, though. He merely sighed, and held her. This time very tenderly.

Tender was nice. She liked tender. In fact, this was the first time anyone had ever held her this way, and she was discovering it was the way she'd like to be held forever.

Forever, and only by Eric.

Which meant... No! It couldn't mean *that*, could it?

She'd been gone thirty minutes, and he still wasn't sure he could leave his office. Just thinking about her made him weak. Got him aroused. Plunged him into the throes of a conflict like he'd never imagined could exist.

But she was short term here in White Elk. That's what she kept saying, and that's what he had to fix on. If he trusted his whole heart to her, could he trust her to stay? She was always so close to running, and he needed stability in his life. The problem was, Dinah didn't think she had stability in her. She did, of course. It was obvious to anyone who looked on. But she fought so hard against it and, truly, he couldn't bring that kind of conflict into his girls' lives. They loved Dinah, and would love her more and more as days turned into weeks, turned into months. She wouldn't hurt them intentionally, he knew that. But the big *what if* still haunted him. What if she did leave? What if he couldn't move forward enough in his life to keep her here?

Moving on… Glancing at the picture of Patricia he still kept on his desk, he smiled wistfully. She'd been important for so long. Maybe longer than had been good for him. He'd taken off the ring, but it was finally time to take off the marriage. Because he wasn't married, and to move forward meant he had to free himself. That was the first step…anything else wasn't being fair to Dinah. And anything else made him feel guilty, made him feel disloyal…*to Dinah*. So he had to move on, or maybe move away from. He wasn't sure which. "And I wish you were here to tell me," he said, picking up the picture.

He studied his wife's face. Beautiful. Angelic. Everything he'd loved. But so long ago, and for the first time in all these years he felt the distance. That's what he'd always feared the most, but somehow it wasn't as bad as he'd thought it would be. Because of Dinah. She was filling that gap. "I'm lonely, Patricia. I need…I need everything again. And I'm at a point in my life when I want it. I'm ready to start over." A lump came to his throat. "Her name is Dinah…Dinah Corday. She's so…so different from the things I thought I had to have in a woman. But she fits.

I'm not sure why, and I'm not even sure she wants to, but these are my first steps, and I'm stumbling because I don't want to lose you… never wanted to lose you. Yet I can't hang on any longer. But even after I took off the wedding ring I still held on because I didn't know if I could move on.

"She's good with the girls, Patricia. She loves them, and they love her. And you'd love her for the way she loves our daughters. This isn't easy for me, though. Until now I've been in limbo because I didn't want to let go, didn't want anything different from what we wanted, but…" He kissed the picture, as he did every day, and sat it back on his desk. As he continued looking at it, though, the image of Dinah's face was beginning to cloud his vision.

After another long moment he picked up Patricia's gold-framed photo, hugged it to his chest, kissed it one final time and laid it gently, face down, in his bottom desk drawer. Then he picked up his phone and dialed.

"Janice, I need a favor. There's something I want you to pick up for me at the hospital. It's in the desk drawer. Take it home, put it away for the girls…"

Afterwards, it wasn't a good feeling settling over him. Wasn't a bad one either. More like it was a necessary feeling. One that had been a long time coming. Because of Dinah.

"Dinah…" He whispered the name as he settled back in his chair, shut his eyes and conjured up her image. So now what was he going to do about Dinah?

CHAPTER NINE

DINAH'S shift at the hospital went quite smoothly. She treated stomachaches, sprains, earache, and a mysterious rash that turned out to be a berry stain. Eric stayed in Emergency as doctor on duty, and every now and then, out of the corner of her eye, she caught him staring at her.

No staring back, though. She was a complete, total mess. Maybe in love. Maybe not. Maybe leaving White Elk. Maybe not. Maybe, maybe, maybe! That was the sum total of her life up until now, and she was only just beginning to see it for what it was. Patterns repeating themselves, over and over. Patterns she ordained because she didn't believe she could get past them. Who knew? This could have been what her subconscious was telling her she deserved, and maybe that's why she simply couldn't let herself go yet again.

Because I...I hide behind excuses. She made mistakes. She was too emotional. She didn't trust. Eric wasn't over his wife. But...they were excuses, and everybody could invent excuses for almost anything they wanted to avoid. And she wanted to avoid... Dear God, it was so simple. *I'm scared of being hurt again.* Her father, her husband, Charles, Molly... Every time she loved, she got hurt. Which was why she was ready to run...because she wanted to avoid the inevitable. To give her heart away, then to have it broken every time...

But Eric wouldn't hurt her. Not intentionally, anyway. Still, his attachment to Patricia... If she forced him to move past that, he would eventually come to resent her. But if he couldn't get past that, their relationship would never be totally theirs.

"Eric, we need to talk," she said, catching up to him in the lobby as the shift ended. She had exactly four hours to sleep then she had to get up and start meal prep at the lodge. But she could make do with three and a half hours of sleep, she felt so strongly about this. They needed to talk. Needed to work this out now, or walk away from each other before they were both hurt too badly. And the one thing she never wanted to do was hurt Eric.

"Sorry, but I'm on my way up to the resort on the middle Sister. They've had an outbreak of food poisoning, and I need to go inspect the kitchen and tend a few patients there. If you'd care to go along…"

So much for good intentions. Dinah declined with a shake of her head. "Don't have time. I've got to be on duty to cook in a little while. But make sure you check the walk-in fridge. In most professional kitchens there's always something lurking in there that should have been thrown out a month ago."

"Wish you'd go with me," he said. "I could make you my unofficial assistant health inspector. But since you can't, can we do this another time?"

She was disappointed, but she understood. His duty as a doctor called, and her duty as a chef wasn't too far behind. "Tomorrow, then?"

"Dinner tonight? I could come to the lodge…"

She shook her head. "I have a dinner meeting to serve. A hundred businessmen coming to eat, drink and be merry. And they have a huge menu ordered."

"So they probably wouldn't notice one more if I just showed up."

She laughed. "They wouldn't, but I would. And I don't need the distraction."

"You're saying I would distract you?"

He took a step closer to her, his eyes full of that familiar devilish glint, which caused Dinah to back up a step. "I'm saying that something might, and it *could* be you." Mercy, why did everything that happened between them have to sizzle so? Because she was positively hot, and in more ways than she knew she could be. And all from such an innocent little suggestion!

"Well, then, I wouldn't want to come between a hundred hungry men and their food, would I?" Grinning, he took another step closer. "Or would I?"

"Only if you're the one who gets to explain why their risotto is dry."

"Nothing worse than dry risotto, I always say. Tomorrow, then? I have an appointment in the morning to look at a house, and a woman's opinion would be nice." Advancing yet another step, he got close enough to her to bend low and whisper, "Especially when you're the woman."

Then he gave her a quick kiss on the neck, and straightened up.

Dinah glanced around to see if anybody had noticed, and when she saw that the only eyes staring at her where those of a gold and white koi swimming in the lobby aquarium, she breathed a sigh of relief. Having this...this whatever it was with Eric in private was one thing. But she didn't want it going public, didn't want people knowing or speculating. That turned it into something it wasn't. Put her in a position she didn't want to be in. Or didn't want to admit to herself that she wanted to be in.

"Did I embarrass you?" he asked, chuckling at her reaction.

"No." Big lie, and Eric realized that, because he was already stepping away from her, a wide grin smeared across his face in his retreat. She did want him to retreat, of course, but part of her didn't want it at all. "Well, maybe a little."

He laughed out loud. "Well, I'm on the verge of embarrassing you even more. So maybe I'd better get going."

"Then I'll see you tomorrow morning," she said, turning and practically running in the opposite direction. She didn't stop until she reached the side entrance door, where she discovered she'd gone to the wrong door, he'd gotten her so flustered. Flustered, confused. What on earth was she doing?

It was a lovely house. Open, spacious. A log cabin, actually, with a vaulted ceiling reaching up so high the only thing Dinah could think about was how to dust the cobwebs off the light fixtures in the ceiling.

She and Eric had said very little on their way inside, but only because the realtor, Robert Tucker, was on their heels, chattering on about every last little detail concerning the house—when it was built, why it was empty, how much land came with it. He was a veritable fountain of facts, probably because he could taste the sale. The minute they stepped through the front door, she saw the look on Eric's face, a look that said he'd come home.

And here she was, trying to figure out a way to dust his home. Even decorate it, fantasizing about a large, overstuffed couch in front of the huge stone fireplace and picturing a king-sized bed in the master suite. Places to curl up and be comfy.

"You like it?" Eric asked.

She liked it so much she could see herself living there. Of course, she wasn't going to gush about it. It wasn't going to be her house. But if she could have chosen the perfect place for her and Eric and the girls, this would have been it. "I think it will be great for you and the girls. The bedrooms are huge. They'll love that. And there's great space out back for them to play. You could put in a swimming pool, maybe their own little playhouse."

"Buying something like this is a big step," he said on a sigh.

"Trepidation's natural. But let the girls have a say in decorating their rooms, and you'll be fine."

"With two five-year-olds in charge, you really think I'll be fine?" He pulled a sheet of paper from his pocket. "This is their list of demands, and it starts with a fenced yard for a dog…a cat, a pony, and a goat."

"A goat?"

Eric shrugged. "Beats an elephant, I suppose."

"And I suppose you'll give in to them."

"On the dog. Maybe the pony."

"But you'll draw the line at a goat? What if the

goat is actually more important to them than the pony or the dog?" she teased.

He chuckled. "You're always on their side, aren't you?"

"It's hard not to be."

"Patricia would have liked that. I always figured she'd be more indulgent with the girls than I would be, and she'd be happy knowing that you're the one indulging them. And that the girls like you. Which they do, Dinah. You're at the top of their best-friends-forever list."

Surprisingly, that touched her, and tears filled her eyes. "Do they ever talk about their mother?" she asked, fighting back the sniffles that were sure to follow.

"Not really. I'm all they've ever had, and I'm not sure I do a good job of keeping Patricia in their lives. I've always been afraid it would make them too sad."

"Or give them part of their identity," she whispered, as the tears finally broke free. "It's a delicate balance, a balance they need."

"What gave you part of your identity, Dinah? What was your delicate balance? Because I want to know you, know what makes you so afraid."

Dinah glanced out the large picture window at Robert Tucker, who was staring back in at them, his face alight with eager anticipation of a sale. She couldn't do this now. Not when he had Patricia on his mind, because he might think she was attacking Patricia, or that she was jealous. Which she was not. Truthfully, she admired the way he loved his wife. But the things she needed to say to him had to be done when Patricia wasn't the first thing he thought about. It had to be about them, with nothing else between them, so it would have to wait. "We don't need to talk about that now. Not when Mr. Tucker is about ready to jump out of his skin. From the look on his face, I think he has plans for the commission he'll make on the sale, and he's anxious to go spend that money."

"Dinah, I do want to talk about it. I want to know…"

She shook her head, thrust out her hand to stop him. Sniffled. Shook her head again. "No. You've got a house to buy. That comes first. For the girls."

"Why do you always do that?"

"What?"

"Act like what you want doesn't matter. Or run away. Because that's what you're doing… running away."

"But right now what I wanted to talk about *doesn't* matter. The house does."

Eric blew out an impatient breath. "You know, you were the one who said you wanted to talk. And I want to listen. But I can't hear you from a distance, Dinah, and that's where you keep yourself."

"Because that's where you want me kept." She hadn't meant that to slip out, but in part that's how she felt.

"Where the hell did you ever get that idea?" he exploded. "I mean, I have issues I'm working through. I'll admit it. I've been stuck in a place that I wasn't ready to leave. But never, ever have I wanted you at a distance. It's you who puts yourself there, who won't let yourself go. Won't let yourself move on. While I've been struggling to find a way to put Patricia in my past and get on with my life, you've been struggling to find a way to stay in the distance. Oh, you get close, move a little forward, but then you retreat. You say you want to talk then you won't. So what am I supposed to do, Dinah?"

"I don't know," she whispered.

"You don't know? After what we've been trying to find for ourselves, that's what it comes down to? You don't know what you want me to do? Or is it that you don't know what you want?"

She looked at Robert Tucker again, and the look on his face was worry now. He feared the loss of his sale.

But Dinah feared the loss of her heart. The first true loss of her heart.

It was so damned frustrating trying to figure her out. He wasn't sure he could, and at this point wasn't sure he wanted to. Granted, the emotional stress of Dinah's last relationship, on top of losing the child she'd come to love, had to be overwhelming. He understood that. Those were things he wanted to help her through, help her overcome. But it was the other thing that frustrated the hell out of him. Dinah was a brilliant, accomplished woman. She had amazing credits as a nurse with skills that surpassed her credits. She had amazing credits as a chef. Plus she was a natural when it came to search and rescue. She was also good with children in a way he'd rarely seen before. Yet she retreated. In fact, she'd almost raised it to an art form, she was so good at it. It was like she'd make her way to the front of the line then immediately remove herself to the rear of it, always on the verge of turning and running away from the line altogether.

He was positive he could see what she wanted. Earlier, when they'd walked through the house he'd decided to buy, the look on her face had been one that said home. She wanted to be there, with him, with the girls, yet when she'd realized that's what she wanted, she'd pulled away. Not just pulled, run as hard and fast as she could. Figuratively. Had they not been in an area of White Elk she didn't know, she'd have probably done her running in the literal sense.

Of course, his own situation didn't help matters any. But at least he was working on it. Trying hard to move forward. Not only for himself but for the girls. They needed more than he was giving them, and Dinah was showing him how much. Oh, not in an overt way—*Eric, do this. Eric, do that.* But she was so tuned in to the girls, so in touch with their needs and how, even at age five, they were growing up. He had to be more sensitive to that, and until Dinah had showed up, he hadn't been aware that he wasn't being responsive the way he needed to be.

"So, what do I do?" he asked Pippa an hour later. She was looking up at him none too patiently.

"Put the flour in the bowl, Daddy! *Just put it in the bowl.*"

They were baking cookies. Or at least trying. The three of them, decked out in aprons, were making a huge mess of Janice's kitchen. Pippa and Paige wanted to bake, but Dinah hadn't been available. So here he was, being the worst cook in the world. But being it with his daughters, at Dinah's suggestion. "Just do it, Eric," she'd told him. "It's about the process, not the results."

And it was a nice process, really. Dinah was right. The experience itself was much better than the cookies would probably be. So why didn't he know that, and why did she?

It was frustrating. He wanted to be a perfect dad. But his shortcomings were mounting. Or maybe he was simply more aware of them now. "Then what comes after the flour?" he asked, truly wishing Dinah was there. It was a wish on his mind more and more because he could see her as the perfect mom to his daughters—the only person he'd thought of that way other than Patricia. But more than being a perfect mom, he could see Dinah as the perfect wife. The wife he wanted.

Paige handed him a measuring spoon. "You measure out the salt, then the baking soda. Be very careful it's only what the recipe says. Dinah says that in baking, you have to be exact."

Amazing, she even sounded like Dinah. "And what happens if I'm not exact?" he teased.

Both girls turned up their noses. "Yuck," they said in unison. Then Pippa continued, "You'd have to throw it out and start all over because it should be the best you can make it."

"And who told you that?" As if he couldn't guess.

"Dinah did," Paige answered. "She said no matter what you do, you have to try your best."

"You two really like her, don't you?"

They nodded eagerly. "But sometimes she's sad," Pippa said. "Why, Daddy?"

"Sometimes people get sad. Even doctors don't always know why. But if I knew how to make Dinah feel better, I would," he said, grabbing the carton of eggs Paige was handing him. "So what do I do with the eggs, and do I put the eggshells into the cookies, too?"

"Daddy!" Both girls giggled, tugged on his apron, tried to push him away from the cabinet.

"You know what?" he said, after a ten minute tussle with the girls. "Let's leave the cookies until later. I'm in the mood to take my two best girls out to a nice dinner."

"At Dinah's restaurant?" Pippa asked.

"At Dinah's restaurant. And you can order off the adult menu. *Escargots*, if you want."

"What's that?" Pippa asked.

"Snails." Eric kept a straight face. "Cooked in garlic butter. Yummy."

"Eew," the both squealed, scampering away to get dressed.

An hour later, dressed in a grey suit he hardly ever wore, escorting two of the prettiest girls in town, one dressed in a lavender A-line dress, one dressed in yellow—the dresses bought on a shopping trip with Dinah—and both wearing colored lip balm she'd also bought them, the Ramsey family made their grand entrance into the Pine Lodge Restaurant, where they were escorted to a table with the best view in the house, as Eric had requested.

"I don't want snails on my menu," Pippa told the maître d'. "Daddy said we could have the adult menu, but it has snails and we don't like snails."

Paige was responding with a firm shake of her head, turning up her nose.

"Very well," the maître d' said, making a big production of handing each of the girls the children's menu. "This is the menu without the snails." He handed the same menu to Eric. "And it's not necessarily for children. We have a very fine chef here who will prepare anything on this menu just the way you like it." He glanced at Eric. "In adult portions, if requested."

"She's going to marry my daddy," Paige said quite loudly.

"Who?" the maître d' asked, as Eric frantically shook his head, trying to stop his daughter from making a pronouncement that shouldn't be made.

"Dinah. The chef. She's going to marry our daddy," Pippa volunteered. "They picked out a house today."

The maître d' responded with the arching of his eyebrows then backed away. "Your server will be Jeffery, and he'll be here momentarily. Please, enjoy your meal." He handed Eric an *adult* menu then left.

"Who told you I'm getting married?" Eric asked, trying to keep his voice down.

"I heard Aunt Janice tell Debbi. She said if you were smart you'd marry Dinah." That from Pippa.

Paige continued, "And you're smart, Daddy. You're the smartest man we know. So that means you're going to marry Dinah!"

"Look, girls. Dinah and I are...friends. We haven't ever..."

"Champagne, sir?" Jeffrey said, setting two flutes of bubbly down in front of Eric. "And for the girls, ginger ale. Compliments of the house, to celebrate your engagement to Miss Corday."

"See, Daddy!" Pippa exclaimed. "Everybody knows."

Eric dropped his head into his hands, and groaned. How could one little dinner with his daughters have gone so wrong, even before the first course?

"So, I hear we're engaged?" Dinah said, stepping up to the table. She was dressed to cook, hair done up under a chef's hat, wearing a white chef's jacket and black and white checkered chef's pants, spatula in hand. "I was just asked if I wanted to step out of the kitchen and have a celebratory flute of champagne with my intended and his family."

"Even she knows," Paige cried. "That means you are!"

Eric's response was to leave his head in his hands and groan again.

Dinner went quite nicely, considering the way it had started. He'd ordered a spinach and squid linguine in garlic cream sauce, from the adult menu, while the girls had chosen chicken, from the children's menu. Except for her one brief appearance at the table, Dinah had stayed in the kitchen. They'd made arrangements for a late-night dessert together after he'd taken the girls home and tucked them into bed. He looked forward to that because it had been Dinah's invitation, the first right and proper date between them, she'd called it. Truth was, they hadn't had that first date yet. Not a real date. Admittedly, he was nervous.

So, after he'd accepted Dinah's offer, he'd explained to the girls that he and Dinah were not picking out a house together, were not getting married. They'd taken the information well, but a mischievous look that had passed between the girls told him the matter was not closed. At least, as far as they were concerned, it wasn't.

Ice cream was the chosen dessert for the girls, while Eric passed on the last course, contented to drink his coffee and stare out the window at the sunset. It was a beautiful evening. Clear. The sun was casting a golden haze over the top of the older Sister, a spectacular sight. This was a good place to live, and he'd never regretted moving here with the girls. Oh, he'd resisted at first, when Neil had suggested it. Neil was from here, and they'd met when Neil had come to California to take a job. Neil's heart had never left here, though, and he'd wanted to come home almost from the day Eric had met him. Somewhere in the middle of Neil's two-year contract, he'd convinced Eric that White Elk would be a good place to raise Pippa and Paige. And, as it had turned out, it had. Now he didn't want to leave here. Didn't have the same desires he'd once had for big-city medicine and an upwardly mobile career. This was good. And finally moving on made it even better.

He *was* moving on, too. Slowly, sometimes not very surely. But he was in the process, thanks to Dinah. She was showing him there was still a lot of life waiting for him if he wanted to have it. With Dinah, he did want to have it. And if nothing else came out of their first right and proper date tonight, he was going to beg…get down on his knees if he had to and beg her patience. The picture of it in his mind was ungainly, but he would do whatever it took to keep her here, to keep her from running away.

For the first time in years, Eric was anxious to see what life held in store for him.

"More sprinkles, please," Pippa said to Jeffrey, who'd inquired as to her satisfaction with the ice cream.

"Me, too," Paige chimed in.

Eric smiled. Yes, it was a very good life. He only wished… Glancing at the kitchen door for the hundredth time that evening, he stopped the thought. No point in wishing. Dinah wasn't ready to step over the line. Wasn't even ready to come close.

He was a patient man, though. Maybe that would be enough to get him through until she had a change of heart. Or maybe that's what would eventually do him in. For now all he had was time…time to wait.

Taking another sip of coffee, he looked out over the mountaintop again, admiring the splendor of the amazing palette of colors against the darkening sky. Johnny Mason's yellow plane, a twelve-passenger commuter, was making its lazy way through the sky. The Canary, everybody called it. The Canary, which was available for rescue and transport whenever he needed it.

Johnny was good that way. So was everybody else here. Nice, solid people. People who cared.

"Can Johnny see us?" Paige asked. "We're almost as high as he is."

"No, it's too far away. And right now Johnny is concentrating on landing." The small airstrip on the middle Sister had been built recently, with two or three small commuters using it regularly, as well as several private planes. During the ski season private planes flew in celebrity skiers practically every day. This evening, though, Johnny was flying in Fallon O'Gara. She was a backbone of the hospital, maybe the most essential person there, and while no one begrudged her a short holiday, he was glad she was coming back. White Elk Hospital simply ran better with Fallon there.

"When can we ride in The Canary?" Pippa asked. "Because Johnny said he'd let us if you will."

Eric chuckled. "He did, did he?"

Both girls nodded.

"We'll talk about it when you're eight."

"Seven," they protested in unison.

"Nine," he argued back.

"Seven and a half," they countered together.

"Ten," he came back one more time.

"Eight," they finally agreed, smiling like the victory was theirs.

Eric took another sip of coffee, thinking what a lucky man he was as he watched The Canary head into its landing. Coming about, it made a sweeping circle and headed directly for the middle Sister then dipped its nose to start its descent. Then, all of a sudden… "Oh, my God!" He dropped his half-full coffee cup on the table, as half the people in the restaurant gasped and screamed. Then he bolted to his feet.

Immediately, Dinah flew from the kitchen. "What is it?" she yelled out over the cries of practically all the people dining there, who were transfixed on what seemed to be nothing outside.

"Plane crash," Eric whispered, hoping the girls hadn't heard. But, of course, they had, for they had their faces pressed to the window, the same way another thirty diners in the restaurant did. "Johnny Mason's plane went down," he choked out, already dialing on his cell phone.

Without missing a beat, Dinah threw her chef's hat onto the table and was untying her apron as she spun around. "I'll be ready to go in two minutes," she called behind her, running as hard and as fast as she could on her way to her room to get ready.

"Neil," Eric said, when his partner answered. "Johnny Mason's plane just went down. As best as I could tell, it's over the landing strip or close to it. I'm already halfway there, so I'm on my way."

Neil agreed to call a full-out rescue, but before he hung up, Eric reminded him, "Fallon's on that plane." It was a sobering thought, yet one he couldn't dwell on as he dialed his sister's number next. "Janice, there's been a plane crash—The Canary's down. I'm up at the lodge on Pine Ridge with the girls and I need you or someone to come and get them."

"Daddy!" Pippa and Paige cried together. "What's wrong? Why are the people yelling?"

"Because there was an accident up on the middle Sister," he said, as he punched in Jess Weldon's number, keeping his fingers crossed that Jess was home and ready to go. Jess had a helicopter, kept it parked in a field behind his house. He was usually ready to go at the drop of a hat. "And they're afraid people might be hurt."

"Are you going to go help the people who might be hurt?" Paige asked.

"Yes, sweetheart, Daddy's going to go help the people."

"Could you have an accident, too, like they did?" Pippa asked. "And get hurt?"

That was the question he never, ever wanted to answer. The reason he'd never told the girls what he did, other than being a doctor. It would scare them, and he didn't want that. It would also raise the inevitable question—the one Pippa had just asked. So he'd avoided the truth, but he'd never lied to the girls, and he wasn't going to start now. "I'm always very careful that I won't get hurt. It could happen, but Daddy's very safe and he doesn't want you to worry about him."

"Aunt Janice does," Paige said.

His girls were so perceptive. It amazed him, scared him and made him proud at the same time. "Look, we'll talk about this when I get back. It'll probably be some time tomorrow. OK?"

Both girls nodded a skeptical, frightened agreement, and Eric pulled them into his arms and hugged them. "We'll finish making those cookies when I get back, and I'll call you later tonight. Promise."

"I'm ready," Dinah shouted, on her way back through the dining room. She was dressed in jeans and boots, wearing a heavy sweater over a T-shirt. Her hair was pulled back into a ponytail, and she was carrying her medical kit, looking every bit the rescuer.

Eric simply stared for a moment. She was in her element, doing this. In her element being a nurse, too. Something about her life had to change and, God willing, he had to be the one to do it. He had to be the one to make her see that she could trust him but, more, that she could trust herself.

Pippa and Paige were left in Jeffrey's capable hands until Janice could get there, and once Eric knew they were going to be fine, he ran to his truck, motioning Dinah to follow.

"Do you know where it went down?" she asked, finally catching up to him. He was already halfway out of his suit, getting ready to change into the clothes he always kept with him in the event of an emergency. While he unbuttoned his shirt, she helped him get the necktie off. While he was pulling off his pants, she was holding out a pair of jeans for him to put on.

"I'm pretty sure he was on his approach to the little landing strip up on the middle Sister. Oh, and Fallon O'Gara was supposed to be flying in. She's been on a holiday in Salt Lake City. Falling in love, I think."

"Oh, no!" Dinah gasped, grabbing Eric's boots for him.

"I talked to her earlier. She said she was going to try and catch the last flight in. Which was Johnny Mason's."

"Maybe it wasn't Johnny's plane that…" She

couldn't bring herself to say "crashed". Plane crashes signified such awful things.

"His plane is yellow, bright yellow. There's no mistaking it."

"Was the plane you saw yellow?"

Eric nodded.

Dinah grimaced. "Since it didn't flame, that's good. Maybe they made the airstrip after all."

"Neil's already had a call from Ella Clark. She runs the landing strip up there. She said the plane's down." He glanced at his watch. "Ten minutes now."

"How long will it take us to get there?"

Eric glanced up as Jess Weldon's helicopter came into view. "A few minutes," he said, bending into the back of the truck, pulling out equipment—ropes, bags, tools.

"The drive would take thirty minutes, this will take less than ten." Eric waved Dinah toward the chopper and led the way, leaving Dinah to run after him, her arms loaded with the supplies he hadn't been able to carry. But when she got to the helicopter, she was surprised to find its pilot stepping out.

"It's a two-seater," Eric yelled. "And I need

you more than I need Jess." He said something
to Jess, tossed him the set of keys to his truck, and
Jess turned and ran toward the parking lot.

"What are you doing?" Dinah practically
screamed, her eyes still fixed on the departing pilot.

"Get in!" He yelled the command then climbed
into the pilot's seat. Blindly, Dinah obeyed, but
once she was strapped in, she shut her eyes and
refused to open them.

"I hope you know what you're doing," she
yelled, gripping the edges of her seat so hard her
knuckles turned white. She could feel the lift,
hear the rotors pick up velocity as they headed
straight up. But she still couldn't look down.
Couldn't even get her eyes open to look, even if
she'd wanted to. "Are you really a pilot, too?" she
shouted. But he didn't answer. So she ventured
a peek in his direction, only to find him talking
into a headset. Before she could close her eyes
again, she caught sight of the ground, saw dozens
of people down there looking up…at them. They
were getting smaller and smaller, which meant…
Dinah gulped hard. Of all the incredible things
not to know about a person, this had to be the
most incredible. Because he was a pilot, an

honest-to-goodness pilot, and a very skilled one judging from the way he handled the aircraft.

"Why didn't you tell me?" she shouted at him when he had finished talking into the headset.

"It never came up," he shouted back.

Her hands loosened their grip a little as they turned and headed for the middle Sister. But she couldn't sit back and relax.

"See if you can spot the crash site," he shouted, then added, "With your eyes open."

"My eyes *are* open." Becoming more and more open all the time. Eric was an amazing man, the man of any sane woman's dreams. Of course, climbing into a helicopter with him might be pushing the sanity point a bit far, but this was a man who kept getting better and better. Maybe the man to make her believe that she *could* believe.

"It's just ahead, but I'm not seeing…"

"They didn't make it," Dinah shouted, practically jumping out of her seat. "I can see it. It's just to the…" She didn't have her bearings. Didn't have a clue which direction was which. "Over there." She pointed.

Eric brought the helicopter round, hovered over the spot for a moment then turned the helicopter in the opposite direction, descending just on the edge of the landing strip. "Watch your head when you get out," he shouted, as they touched down. "Give the rotors a minute…"

The words fell on deaf ears. Dinah bolted out, grabbed her medical bag and a few of Eric's tools, and took off running across the end of the landing strip, heading into what was, essentially, a cleared area at the base of an old ski slope that had shut down years ago, when the Cedar Ridge Lodge had been built on the other side of the mountain. No one was up there yet, except a single truck she saw ahead of her. It was parked off the gravel road, its driver's door open.

"Dinah," Eric called, from behind, running hard to catch up to her.

"I can see it, Eric." But not for long, as it was getting dark. And that didn't bode well for the rescue, if the victims weren't all contained in a small area.

He caught up to her, and they paused together at Ella's truck. Looked. Then, as if there was an unspoken agreement between, ran to the crash site, Dinah going to the left, Eric to the right.

"Full plane," Ella cried. She was on her hands

and knees next to a passenger, feeling for a pulse. "I called it in."

Dinah dropped to her knees beside the woman, but Ella gave her a grave shake of the head. "I don't think this one will be needing your services this evening."

After she'd confirmed what the old woman already knew, Dinah stood back up, looked around. Saw someone sitting up, way off to the side of the crash. "Are you going to be OK?" Dinah asked Ella.

"I've been running one airstrip or another for fifty years. Sorry to say, this isn't my first crash. I'll be fine."

The next two people Dinah checked were injured, but stable enough. And grateful to be alive. But she came upon the pilot, at least she assumed him to be a pilot because he wore a bright yellow T-shirt with the word *Pilot* across his chest in blue. Except *Pilot* was covered in bright red blood, and poor Johnny had no pulse. In a quick assessment, Dinah counted three serious conditions, and her stomach roiled. Johnny had a puncture wound to the thigh that was leaking a fair amount of blood, a gash to his head which had rendered him unconscious, and a huge bruise to the chest, which was going to be the injury she had to fight hardest. Death was never easy, and she didn't like losing to it. It wasn't inevitable for Johnny, though.

"Dinah!" Eric shouted from somewhere on the other side of the wreckage. "Are you OK?"

"I'm fine! Doing CPR," she shouted back. She was starting chest compressions now, hoping it would be enough. "What's the estimated arrival on anybody getting here?"

"Ten minutes tops."

Ten minutes. She could do this for ten minutes. But what if someone else here needed those ten minutes, too? "Then I'll be good over here."

"Do you need anything?" he shouted.

Other than their first right and proper date? It seemed something always got in the way, that they always had more important things to do. What an amazing team they made. A team…she'd never thought of her and Eric in those terms. "I'm good. Oxygen would be nice as soon as we get it up here, though." Yes, they were an amazing team. Maybe with some kinks to work out. But amazing, all the same. "Well, Mr Pilot," she said to Johnny

Mason. "You'd better make this worth my while, because it's just you and me for the next ten minutes, and I don't want you letting me down in the end. I have expectations, and you'd better not ruin them for me. You hear?"

Expectations. She looked across the crash site as Eric was about to climb through the plane wreckage. Yes, she did have expectations. "It's just you and me," she whispered. You and me, meaning Eric and herself.

CHAPTER TEN

"NEED some help with that?"

Dinah looked up, saw the silhouetted shadow of a large, looming mountain man. To her, he looked like a grizzly bear.

"You know CPR?" she asked him, wondering where he'd come from.

"In my clean-shaven days I was Dr. Walter Graham, obstetrician. Formerly a full-time doctor at the White Elk Hospital and currently part-time when I take a notion to work. In my unshaven days, I'm Walt. I was up on the overlook, getting ready to hike down the other side, when I saw the plane come down." He knelt, nudged Dinah aside and assumed his place doing CPR. "You're faster than I am, can get to more people. You go on. Johnny and I will be fine here."

"Rescue crew should be up here any time

now." She grabbed her medical bag and stood. "Call me if you need something." Then she ran for the crushed fuselage, wondering if Eric was still inside. But halfway there, the faint call of someone in the distance caught her attention, so she stopped, listened. Couldn't pinpoint it.

"Hello," she called. "Can you answer me?"

There was no response.

"Can you tell me where you are?"

Again, no response. The only sound she could hear was the crunching of truck tires on the gravel road. Help was here but, damn, she really needed silence. Really needed to be able to hear. "Hello?" She tried one more time then held her breath, hoping, praying…

A faint moan, coming from somewhere to the side of the crash site. But where, exactly? "Eric, over here. I've got someone over here and I can't find them."

No time to wait for the portable lights to be set up, no time to wait for the rescuers to be organized. Dinah dashed off to the wooded area on the edge of the clearing, and started her search. "I'm coming," she called out. "Don't give up. I'm on my way."

"Dinah, where are you?" Eric called.

"Just at the tree line," she yelled back, flashing her light in the direction of his voice. "I heard someone moaning."

"Any other response?" he asked, once he'd caught up to her.

"No. And it was just the one moan. I mean, it could have been an animal, but… Is everybody accounted for at the site? All the victims?"

"Everybody but Fallon. And there's some confusion about whether or not she took the flight. It turns out that Johnny had her on the manifest for tomorrow morning. Her cell phone is off, but we're trying to contact her friends right now."

"Then she could be out here."

"And we'll find her if she is." For the next few minutes they made their way slowly through the underbrush, pushing back branches, climbing around bushes, in places practically dropping to their knees to crawl, the undergrowth was so dense. They stayed apart, not talking but close enough to see one another, except Dinah couldn't look at him. Because to look was to admit her feelings. And to admit them was to change everything.

But changing because she was in love? That wasn't such a bad thing, was it?

After all, she did love Eric in a way she'd never known. Not with anybody, ever.

"One small step," she whispered. But, really, wasn't it more like one gigantic leap of faith?

"Eric, come in," Neil radioed from the crash site. "We've heard about Fallon."

He clicked on his radio. "What?"

"She was on the plane. And she's not one of the victims. We have eleven, not including the pilot. One fatality and ten survivors, three of them critical, one extremely critical, six stable. Fallon's not one of them and we've looked everywhere inside the grid we laid out. She's not here, and there's nothing to suggest she's buried in the actual plane wreckage somewhere."

Eric stood up, brushed the dirt off his knees. "Then she's here somewhere, where Dinah said she was."

"I'll get another team in to you right away," Neil said, then clicked off.

"Fallon," Dinah called from somewhere off to his left.

"I think so."

"No, it's Fallon. I've found her."

He didn't want to ask. Didn't want to know.

"She's alive, Eric. Unconscious, pretty badly injured, but alive."

In mere seconds he was at Dinah's side, assessing the pupils of Fallon's eyes. "Responsive," he said, so relieved he nearly went weak at the knees.

"Can't get a blood pressure on her," Dinah said, and immediately started probing Fallon's belly. "It's rigid. Probably internal bleeding."

Eric was checking for bone injuries and gaping wounds. "No compound fracture, but I think she's got several facial fractures, probably a shoulder fracture…can't tell about her neck and spine."

"Eric." Dinah leaned in close to him. "She's losing her airway. Her breath sounds are diminishing pretty quickly."

"Damn," he muttered, immediately putting a stethoscope to her lungs. Dinah was right. Her breathing was being compromised…shutting down. But before he could say anything, Dinah was already pouring an iodine scrub on Fallon's throat—an iodine scrub he kept in his medical bag.

"You have a blade?" she asked him, as he took Fallon's pulse.

"In the pocket on the right side." He bent closer to Fallon. "You stay with me, you hear? It's going to be a rough one, but I'm going to pull you through it…Dinah and I are going to pull you through it, Fallon. And what we have to do now is trach you…" Cut a hole in her windpipe to allow her to breathe. "You've got too much swelling in your trachea, but hang in there with me. We'll get you to the hospital in just a few minutes and get some pain meds into you."

Dinah handed the scalpel over to Eric, and squeezed his hand at the same time. Without a word, she poised herself with a flashlight, ready to provide light for the procedure, but Neil arrived with several volunteers, who all carried flashlights and spotlights. And in the blink of an eye, Eric had performed the life-saving procedure, sliced a tiny hole into Fallon's throat, through the skin, through the cartilage. With no time to spare.

"She's going to be fine," Dinah whispered, as Neil handed her a plastic tube to insert into the tiny incision Eric had made in her throat.

Eric glanced over at her, too overcome to speak. What they did together…professionally, it was a perfect fit. But personally…yes, he would definitely get down on his knees to beg Dinah's patience with him. "I'm glad you were here," he said, his voice rough. Maybe beg more while he was down there.

"Well, I seem to be getting better at emergency rescue."

"Not for that," he said. "For me. I'm glad you were here for me."

It took fifteen more minutes to stabilize Fallon for transport, fifteen minutes getting the IV in her vein, getting oxygen started. Fifteen minutes trying not to look at the facial fractures, the cuts, the unknown conditions that could only be diagnosed in the hospital. But she was alive, and that's what Eric kept telling himself as his team stabilized her neck and strapped her to the stretcher.

Rescue was always personal, but never this personal. And he was drained, physically and emotionally.

"She's going to make it," Dinah reassured him, slipping her arm around his waist. "I know she's in rough shape right now, but she's going to pull through."

"That was a good call on her breathing," he said, leaning in, savoring her physical support as much as her touch.

"And that was pretty slick work, getting her airway opened up so quickly." She leaned her head into his side. "We're good together, aren't we?"

"Perfect." So now that he knew, without a doubt, what he wanted, all he had to do was figure out how to make it happen. What would it take to convince Dinah to bridge the distance she always drew between them? *Bridge it permanently.* "Look, will you do me a favour? I'm going to stay here and clean up the site. Pick up the trash, make sure we're not leaving any equipment behind. Do you mind going to Pippa and Paige? They were too close to this, and I don't want them to be scared. I'll call them when I get out of here and get cell phone reception, but I'd feel better knowing you're with them until I can get home. Janice is good, but even the girls recognize that she gets nervous. Right now, as they saw the plane, and I'm sure they've heard all about it, I'd like you to—"

"You don't have to ask, Eric. I'm on my way." She stood on tiptoe and kissed his cheek. "Too bad you haven't moved into your new house, because I saw a Jacuzzi there, and that would sure be a nice place for us to relax once the girls are asleep for the night."

"Damn," he groaned. "That's the best offer I've had in years, and I have no way of taking you up on it."

"Not now you don't. But maybe in a while…"

"Do you mean that, Dinah?"

"I want to mean it, Eric. I really want to mean it. But it's not easy to admit, not easy to do, and my life is still a mess…"

That distance again… Damn, what was he going to do? Rather than trying to find the impossible answer, he pulled her roughly to his chest, breaking that distance, if only for the moment, and kissed her hard and fast on her lips, then pushed her away. "We'll continue that later, but I want you going down the mountain with the team now. OK?"

She kissed her fingertips, dirty as they were, and brushed them across his lips. "OK." Then she trotted down the trail after the rest of the team.

Eric kept the flashlight trained on her until she was out of sight then he began the clean-up. Truth was, he could have come back in the morning. There was no great hurry to get this done. But right now he wanted to be alone. He had a lot of thinking to do. And he needed to do it now.

"I was just checking on Fallon, and she's in pretty bad shape," Dinah whispered to Janice. Pippa and Paige were busy in the kitchen, making sandwiches for Eric. Ten sandwiches and counting, made out of every conceivable thing from the kitchen that could be slapped between two pieces of bread. Including the cookie dough. "We lost one, several are critical, most are stable, though."

"Which is a blessing," Janice said. "Although, I'm so sorry for the one who didn't make it." She glanced at the pendulum clock on the wall. "How long before he'll be home?"

"Actually, I thought he'd be here by now." It had been only two hours, and maybe it was merely her eagerness to be in his arms that had protracted those hours into an interminable length. "But who knows? Maybe he's taking some of the equipment back to the hospital, or even checking on some of the victims who'll be treated there? He's probably in the emergency room right now, totally unaware of the time."

"He needs someone to make him aware," Janice said. "Don't get me wrong. I've been happy having him here, and I love Pippa and Paige. But they need another life…all of them. And I…well. So do I. I'm not getting any younger, and there's this really nice man who owns a little café across the street from my shop. We have lunch together a couple times a week, and we've even gone out in the evenings. Yet…"

"You haven't been able to bring him home."

Eric's sister shook her head. "My daughter, Debbi, has a life. She's decided to go to Chicago next month, after she graduates from high school, and one of Gabrielle's friends there is going to make sure she doesn't get herself into too much trouble. Which means I'll be alone for the first time in eighteen years. And I'm looking forward to it. Though I'll be sad to see her go, sad to see Eric and the twins go, too."

"Sad, but not sad."

"Does that sound terrible, Dinah?"

"It sounds normal. And you deserve it."

"But I worry, because Eric is so caught up in the past. And I want him to move on with his life. This house he's buying is a good thing, and I have an idea it has something to do with you. So does his taking off his wedding band, and finally putting Patricia's photo away."

"Her photo?"

"The one on his desk at work. He called me the other day, had me come and take it."

Dinah had seen him stare at that photo so often, seen that distant look in his eyes when he did. These changes couldn't be easy for him, and yet he did them so quietly, and with so much strength. Not like her, making her changes kicking and screaming and being so resistant. Even tonight, when he'd asked her if she meant it…the Jacuzzi with overtones of so much more…she hadn't said she meant it. She'd said she was *trying* to mean it. Then said it wasn't easy. Wasn't easy… In truth, it was the easiest thing she'd ever done, falling in love with Eric. And the instant he walked through that door, she was going to tell him so.

* * *

"Still no word?" Dinah asked one of the rescuers who was still lingering in the hospital, helping to get all the plane crash patients settled in. It had been four hours and she was pacing the emergency department halls now, making a nuisance of herself.

"He's fine, Dinah. Sometimes Eric likes to unwind after these things. He's gone off before. Don't worry." George Fitzhenry, one of team leaders, squeezed her shoulder. "He's had a lot on his mind and sometimes you simply need to get away to think."

"I suppose you're right." George knew Eric's habits, and he wasn't concerned. So she shouldn't be concerned either. She was, though. Everything in her screamed she had to be concerned. "But he was anxious to get back to Pippa and Paige."

"And he knows they're in bed by now. I think it's too soon to be so worried. Eric will turn up when he's ready."

"But couldn't we do some kind of preliminary search?"

George shook his head. "It's too soon. People haven't even gotten home from the last effort.

But if he hasn't called or come back in another hour or two, we'll look for him. Right now it's better to wait."

"Sure," she said, starting to turn away. But the voice screaming in her head wouldn't let her turn away. *Trust yourself, Dinah! Trust yourself!* That voice wouldn't let her be talked out of what she felt, what she knew. *Trust yourself, Dinah.* Eric's life depended on that! "He's in trouble, George. You're wrong about this, and we do need to be worried. Something's wrong, and I'm going back out there to look for him. I'll need someone with me so I'm going to go find Neil and tell him to call a rescue. *Now.*"

After Dinah found Neil, and demanded action, he shut the patient chart he'd been writing in, retracted the point on his pen then tossed both pen and chart on the desk. "I'll have a team ready in twenty minutes."

Twenty minutes…too long. But going out there alone was stupid. Eric would be the first one to tell her so. Now it was a matter of fighting her will, because everything inside her wanted to run for the door and not look back. The deeper sense inside her, though, the sense Eric had put there, was holding her back, forcing her to finally do this the right way. Because it was Eric's life on the line. Eric… "I'll be waiting." Waiting the longest wait of her life.

Neil ran the effort without a hitch. A dozen people were at the hospital door in a matter of minutes, still dirty from the night's earlier rescue, ready to go back out, ready to find Eric. In those few minutes while she waited, Dinah tried his cell phone over and over. Tried to get through to Ella Clark, to see if Eric's truck, driven there earlier by Jess Weldon, was still there, but Ella wasn't answering. Neil said she took off her hearing aid at night.

Various people from town called in, all reporting no sign of him. Apparently, there was a foot search going on. People were walking the streets, looking for his truck. Not that Eric was the type who would be so irresponsible as to simply wander off this way. He wouldn't, and Dinah was biting her nails with worry. "The first thing I'm going to do when we find him is hug him and tell him how much I love him," she said on the cell phone to Angela. "The second thing I'm going to do is…tell him again how much I love him."

"He's going to be fine," her sister reassured her. "He probably has a flat tire."

Or he'd fallen off the side of a mountain somewhere. "Look, I'll call you. Neil's got everybody ready to go out so I've got to run." And run was what she did. To the truck, to climb into the front seat with Neil. To the site where they'd last seen his truck at the landing strip the instant Neil had stopped his own truck. To the place in the woods where they'd found Fallon, to make sure he'd cleaned the site. Which he had. By the time Neil had caught up with her, she already knew everything there was to know at that particular site. Eric wasn't there.

"I have people tracking him down the road," Neil explained. "Driving it, taking the side roads. Walking it, to look for any indication of where he might have gone over."

"And that's it? That's all we can do?"

"Eric's not given to doing stupid things. He knows how to leave signs if he's in trouble, and he knows how to take care of himself until we can get to him."

Words meant to calm her down, but it wasn't working. "Look, I'm going to get out and walk down the main road like the others are doing. Maybe I'll see something..." She shrugged. "Maybe I won't, but at least I'll be doing something other than sitting." Something was better than nothing.

So she climbed out of Neil's truck and began her descent down the road leading away from the middle Sister, thinking about the Ute Indian legend. If ever there was a time when the Three Sisters needed to protect someone in their shadows, this was it. Looking up to the oldest Sister, which towered over this, the middle Sister, she prayed for the three of them to work their magic, and work it fast.

Rescuers in front of her, sweeping the road with their flashlights, walked slowly, looking everywhere. It was a methodical search as they hunted two by two, darting off the road into the underbrush every now and again then returning to the road, dejected. Coming up behind them, having a second look at everything the way she was, was probably a waste of time, but she was trying to think like Eric now. He had been going to clean up and go to the girls. He might have been in a hurry... Had the girls called him? Or had he called the girls, like he'd promised? Flipping open her phone, she wondered. "Hello, Janice," she said when Eric's sister answered.

"Did you find him?" Janice choked.

"No, not yet. But we've got a dozen people out on the mountain, and at least that many in town. There's a good chance he's had trouble with his truck." No one knew that, no one had even speculated, but Janice needed to hear something reassuring, although Dinah wasn't sure if she'd said it for Janice's sake or for her own. "But what I need to know is if he called the twins. I remembered him telling me that he'd call them when he got out of here, so I was wondering…"

"Just a minute," Janice interrupted, then dropped the phone. Almost immediately, she was back on. "He did call them. Told them he was on his way home, and to get the cookie dough ready."

"And that's all?"

"That's all they said, except they wanted more chocolate chips."

Wanted more chocolate chips. The words kept coming back to her, nagging, not letting go, for the next several minutes on her trek down the road. More chocolate chips… "Neil," she said when she called him on his cell phone. "If I were on the middle Sister and wanted to go and find a bag of chocolate chips, where would I go?"

"What the hell are you talking about, Dinah?" he snapped.

"Chocolate chips. Where would be the best place to find them on my way home from the middle Sister?"

"Is there a point to this?"

"I don't know…maybe." Would he have gone for chocolate chips?

"You'd go to Bertie's Convenient Store, open all night. At the fork, halfway down the main road, you'd take the road to the west, go about a mile, and if you knew the short cut, you'd come to the giant boulder—it looks like an old lady with a crooked nose—and take the dirt road around it…more like a wide, dirt path."

"Would Eric know the short cut?" she asked.

"Would Eric have gone to Bertie's for chocolate chips?" Neil asked, gunning his engine. Before Dinah could answer his question, he'd pulled up alongside her. "Get in," he said, barely stopping.

She was in, door not quite shut when he took off, but not before he'd radioed his position to several of the rescue team. "It makes as much sense as anything else does." Dinah fastened her seat belt. "Everything he does is for the girls, and if they wanted chocolate chips, I think he'd go out in a blizzard to get them."

"Well, apparently he's more predictable for you than he is for me, because there's no way I'd have put chocolate chips together with him going missing."

"Let's hope he's predictable this time." Gripping the side of the seat as Neil took the turn at the fork, all she could do was stare out the window, hoping to see something…anything. But all she saw was a dark, nearly starless night, where glowing eyes stared out from their bushy hiding places, and bugs darted in and out of the truck's headlights. Truth was, there was nothing to see. Without light it was hopeless. But waiting until morning was unthinkable. Neil knew that, every rescue worker out on the hunt knew that. Yet they were there, doing what they had to do, breaking Eric's own rules about this kind of night search, to find Eric. "So, how much farther to this boulder?"

Neil lifted his hand from the steering wheel at

the same moment he stepped on the brake and pointed to it. "Right there."

In the night shadows, it did resemble the profile of an old woman with a hooked nose. "Should we drive, or walk?"

"Eric's truck is heavier than mine so he might have gone this way. But I can't drive it because after all the rains and flooding we've had recently, my truck will get bogged down." He stopped the truck directly under the old woman's nose. "So we'll walk for a while and see what we can find."

Words said to no one, as Dinah was already on her way out the door.

Together, they walked about half a mile down a rutted, muddy path, slipping and sliding, most of the time hanging on to each other to keep themselves upright. "The tracks look fresh," Dinah said, shining her flashlight on the road.

"Kids in town like to come down this way. They use it for a lovers' lane."

"Well, it's isolated enough." Too isolated, she thought, while trying to extricate her boot from a particularly deep rut...one that looked like it could open up and swallow the whole town of White Elk. Stopping, she bent to help her foot slip back into the boot and dropped her flashlight. It plopped, more than rolled, and its beam fixed on a little grassy patch off to the side of the road. She didn't pay attention until after she'd got her boot back on and was going to get her flashlight. That's when she saw it. A pink shoelace.

Dinah gasped. "He's here," she whispered, then immediately yelled, "Eric, can you hear me? Eric!"

"Eric!" Neil yelled, not sure why or how Dinah had decided this was the place. But he yelled again, and began frantically sweeping his light from one side of the road to the other.

"Eric," Dinah yelled again. "Where are you?" She grabbed up the shoelace, tucked it into her pocket, and studied the spot for a moment. "I think the tracks are his," she said, looking on down the road, still seeing nothing. "I think he came this way, something happened, and he tossed a pink shoelace out the window as a sign."

"A pink shoelace?"

"Long story," Dinah said, moving on ahead in mud halfway up to her knees now. Neil was flanking her on the right, keeping his distance and keeping his eyes peeled for anything on that side of the road. But Dinah was the one who found it…found the spot about three hundred yards away when the tire marks veered off… "Here," she choked, running straight into the waist-high prairie grass, following tracks that had flattened the grass. "Eric, can you hear me?"

In response, a honk. Which brought immediate tears of relief as she followed the trail until it came to the overturned vehicle. It was on its side. Lights still on, shining into the trees. "Eric," she choked, dropping to the ground to look into the cab.

He smiled at her. Cut, bloody. Half-strangled by the seat belt. Beautiful. "I thought you'd never get here," he choked, his voice hoarse.

Well, the first thing she wanted to do—hug him—wasn't going to happen right now. He was too injured. A quick assessment revealed a broken leg, as best she could tell without moving him. Probably a dislocated shoulder, too. So no hugs from her. But in her heart she was hugging him forever. However, the second thing she'd said she'd do… "I love you," she whispered, crawling in and cutting away the seat belt while Neil radioed their location to his teams. Muddy tears were streaking down her cheeks. "I love you more than anybody I've ever loved in the whole world, and if you ever do this to me again, I'll…" She sniffled, cut through the shoulder part of the seat belt, and pulled away the remnants of the air bag which Eric had already punctured and deflated.

"You'll what?"

"I'll love you more than anybody I've ever loved in the whole world."

He was coming home today. It had been a crazy seven days, subduing the twins who would have surely injured Eric in their enthusiasm to hug him, and trying to get his house ready so he wouldn't have to go home to Janice's cottage. He was going to need a medical bed for a while, and she'd had it set up right in the front room of his new cabin. Dr. Kent Stafford, one of White Elk's full-time orthopedic surgeons, had actually recommended Eric to a rehab facility for a couple of weeks, but Eric had refused. Said he wanted to be with his girls. Said over and over he wanted to be with Dinah.

So she was busy making sure that would happen.

As it turned out, he *had* been going after chocolate chips that night. In a hurry. Taking the short cut. His truck had slipped out of control in the mud, the brakes wouldn't hold it, and it had picked up speed in its descent. On a flat surface, nothing would have happened. But rolling down the side of a foothill… The Three Sisters had been watching over him because, by rights, he should have been killed.

And the pink shoelace…he'd tossed it out the window when he'd realized he was going to take a long, bumpy ride to the end.

"In the middle of the front room?" Those were Eric's first words when the medic rolled him in the door. His broken leg, now in a cast, was elevated. A pink cast at Pippa and Paige's insistence. He was shirtless, but the brace supporting four broken ribs covered most of his chest. And his arm was in a sling. A mess, but such a handsome mess that tears welled in Dinah's eyes.

"In the middle of the room," she said, smiling so widely it almost hurt.

"I was hoping for some privacy."

She waved to George Fitzhenry, who'd brought him home and was on his way back out. "In your condition, Eric, privacy's the last thing you need. Especially if you're thinking what I think you're thinking."

Eric sighed. "So how are you going to lift me into bed?"

"I have a few friends coming by later. And you're getting a full-time nurse. Hired the best one I could find."

"That would be you."

"That would be me. And I'll be full-time nurse at White Elk Hospital as soon as my private duty is over."

"Meaning?"

"You know what it means."

"But I want to hear you say it. No, I need to hear you say it."

Yes, he did, and she wanted to say it to him. "I'm going to stay, Eric—here in White Elk, here with you and the girls. With my sister. *I want to stay here.*"

"Do you know how good that sounds?"

"It couldn't sound any better to hear it than it feels to say it. Because it's what I truly want to do. I mean, I kept telling myself that if I walked away from everything I'd found here in White Elk I'd be fine. Better to be alone, keep myself hidden, than open myself up to getting hurt again. I wanted you so much, but I was scared… scared I wasn't enough, scared I'd let you down, scared you'd be disappointed. So it was easier to push you away, even run away…"

"To Costa Rica?" he said, smiling.

"It was never about running to someplace. It was always about running away from something…in this case, you."

"But I wouldn't have hurt you, Dinah."

"Not intentionally. But what happened if we woke up one morning and you decided that I wasn't…"

"Patricia?"

She nodded. "And the thing is, it wasn't even about Patricia. I'm so glad you had her, so glad you had such a wonderful marriage with her. I just didn't feel like I could be enough for you after you've already had perfection. For me, it's always easy to hide behind excuses, which is what I've been doing, Eric. The men in my life leave, I'm too emotional to be a nurse, Charles betrayed me…excuses. And I wanted to turn you into another excuse. But you wouldn't let me. And I know I was forcing you into that position by distancing myself, as you called it. Getting close then shoving you away. Even resigning from the hospital."

"I would have come after you, Dinah. Don't you know that I've been trying to figure out all along how to keep you here, or what to do if you did run away?"

"You were?"

"Of course I was. I mean, I've made a mess of things myself, and I know that. So maybe I've kept myself at some of that distance I've accused of you keeping while I was trying to figure out a way to make this work between us. I was always afraid that Patricia would be an issue…"

"I understand your feelings for her, Eric."

"An issue for you, Dinah. I never wanted you to think I was comparing you, or putting you second. But when you love someone it's hard to let go. Which is why I wasn't going to let go of you no matter what happened. Even if I had to go all the way to Costa Rica to get you."

"You would have?"

"I would have," he said.

A shuddering sigh over took her. "I loved Molly, and that day when she died, when I kept holding on to her…I couldn't bear the pain. That's why I left nursing. As much as I loved, it just hurt so much, and there was nothing I could do. Molly was going to die and I knew that, but I think I blocked it from my mind because when it happened…I went to pieces, Eric. I went to pieces, and how can you be a good nurse if you get that emotional?"

"The best nurses and doctors do get that involved, Dinah. Loving someone that deeply is never anything to be ashamed of, and hurting when you lose them is natural. You loved a little girl who desperately needed someone in this world to love her, and the Dinah I know will do that again and again because that's what makes her extraordinary…as a person, as a nurse."

She paused for a moment, shut her eyes, fighting back the tears. "When Charles pulled me away, physically restrained me and had me sedated, I'd never felt more betrayed…more pain in my life. He told me I was being an idiot, opening myself up to being hurt, that what I was suffering was my fault. That I was weak."

"Loving someone never makes you weak,

Dinah. It's what makes you strong. Builds you up. Makes you better."

"But I was so wounded, and I just didn't want to…to bleed that way anymore. My father, my husband, my fiancé, Molly… I convinced myself it was easier living life alone. That maybe Charles was right."

"He was wrong, and it's not easier. I've been alone for years and I think I'd convinced myself of the same thing, that it's easier that way. And it wasn't the pain I was running from so much as it was the fear of starting over. I'd had everything I'd ever wanted in life then lost so much of it, and for me it just became easier not to want any of it again. I had my work, my girls… By all standards, that makes me a very lucky man. Then I met you, and…"

"I made you miserable."

"Sometimes, because I had to reevaluate where I was and what I was doing, and, as you've seen, I've been pretty resistant to that. But you also made me incredibly happy, and I don't think I ever counted on having that kind of happiness again. Or maybe I'd convinced myself I didn't need it. And to be honest, I did feel guilty…not because of Patricia, or moving away from Patricia. I felt guilty because I wasn't feeling guilty, if that makes any sense. All along I think I expected some huge blanket of guilt to drop down and smother me if I ever looked at another woman…thought of another woman the way I have you. Maybe I even counted on it happening so I wouldn't have to move on with my life. Then, when that didn't happen, when I realized that I was getting happier, I wasn't sure how to handle it."

"Well, we're quite the pair, aren't we? Me running away from the things I love most because I'm afraid of getting hurt, you hiding because you're afraid of being happy. You know, I wanted you to let me down, Eric. I fought like hell to make you do it so I didn't have to face myself, and I fell more and more in love with you each and every time you wouldn't be pushed too far."

"I know."

His voice was so gentle it melted her heart. "Every time I did, I wanted you to come and get me. And every time I was so afraid you would, and even more afraid you wouldn't."

"I know that, too."

"And you still want someone as crazy as me raising your daughters?"

"Crazy's good," he said. "As long as it's crazy in love."

"And I am, Eric. I fought myself and lost miserably. Which means I've won everything."

"Damn, I wish you could be sitting in my lap," he said. "Because I want to show you how crazy in love feels."

"You can't even put your arms around me," she said, sniffling. "But I can put my arms around you…a little bit. If you trust me to do that without hurting you." Crossing over to his wheelchair, Dinah bent down and eased her arms around him, barely touching him. But it was a good touch. *A perfect touch*. "Thank you, Eric. You've given me everything, and I don't know how to repay you."

"Marry me?" he asked, quite simply. "I know this isn't the most romantic proposal, and just let me warn you that if you say yes, we're going to do it as soon as we get the license, even with me in this pink leg cast, because I don't want to spend another day of my life without you. Also be warned, the girls already have the wedding planned. They've been working on it for days, and I think their intent is to upstage us."

She started crying again. "It sounds beautiful…perfect." She backed away for fear she'd hurt him, and propped herself against the hospital bed.

"It was a long time coming, trying to forget Patricia."

"But you don't have to forget her, Eric. She was such an important part of your life…of the lives of three of the people I love most in this world. She took care of you, loved you, gave you two amazing children, and for that I love her, too. So you shouldn't forget her…none of us should."

"When I fell in love with you, that's what I came to realize. It wasn't about forgetting her. I loved Patricia with all my heart, and that won't change. But I learned my heart has room to love someone else, too…love someone else with all my heart. And that's how I love you, Dinah. That day in the rain, when you fought with me, it was like I woke up for the first time in many years. Woke up, felt alive. Then every time after that… There were so many things in me that I'd put away. Things you reminded me were still there. And I want that with you, Dinah, all of it."

"You don't mind pink shoelaces, do you? And pink and purple walls in the girls' bedrooms? Because we've already talked about it and it's a unanimous decision. Pippa's walls will be pink on the top half, purple on the bottom, and Paige's walls will be purple on the top half, pink on the bottom. Not negotiable. The goat is negotiable, though. But not the pony or the dog." She smiled. "Although I can think of some things I'd love to negotiate on my own. Like a honeymoon, *without the girls*, once you're healed."

"Care to tell me what you have in mind for that honeymoon?"

"And get you all excited? That could hurt a man in your condition."

"My only condition is totally, incurably in love."

"Well, in that case…" She bent over and gave him a circumspect kiss on the forehead.

"Not good enough."

Another one on the tip of his nose.

"Not good enough."

One on each cheek.

"Closer, but still not good enough."

This time she kissed him on the lips. Tenderly, and rather quickly. But there would be time for more. A lifetime for more. "Oh, and so you'll know," she whispered in his ear, "I'm taking over your duties with the rescue team. I think I have a knack for it."

"You're not trained for it."

"I'll get my training."

"But you're getting married, going to be a mother, going to be a nurse…"

Dinah gave him a broad smile, folded her arms across her chest, and looked down at him. "Trust me, I know what I'm doing."

"You know, you're sexy when you talk that way. I like a woman who knows what she's doing." He arched wicked eyebrows.

"Staying with the man I love is what I'm doing," she said, taking his face in her hands and going straight for his lips this time. "For the rest of my life."